TROPIC ANGEL

A LUKE ANGEL THRILLER

NATE VAN COOPS

Skylighter
Press

ONE

GEAR UP

A GOOD PILOT doesn't show sweat.

Come what may, the captain of an aircraft keeps their shit together.

Barry Sutherland was soaking the seat cushion. Droplets had turned into a steady trickle down the back of his neck and I could tell things up in the flight deck were headed in the wrong direction.

It was a typical sauna of a Florida afternoon, but Barry's growing dampness in the pilot seat had nothing to do with the humidity and everything to do with this being our third time around the traffic pattern with the landing gear stuck up.

I was along on this pre-purchase inspection flight as Barry's mechanical advisor. He'd scoured Trade-a-Plane and every other online aircraft sales site for weeks and had been so thrilled to find an aircraft in his price range that he couldn't wait to pull the chocks and fly it.

I'd advised him to do the inspection first and the flight after, and today was turning out to be a memorable example as to why.

So much for advice.

The plane's owner, a big guy named Keith, was in the co-pilot seat and his continual protestations that the gear had worked just fine on the way down from Georgia were falling on deaf ears.

Barry cast occasional glances back at me for help, but buckled into a rear-facing club seat of the Piper Seneca II, I wasn't in a place to do anything about its landing gear. Maybe he thought I could climb under the wings like Spider-Man and dismantle the problematic gear door.

That's what I figured the issue was anyway. Something was jammed and no amount of dumping the emergency gear extension valve had done a thing to budge it. Might even have made our situation worse if the throbbing veins on Keith's forehead said anything about it. He was a heavy dude, mid-sixties, forearms like melons. If the stress kept up, he might have a coronary.

I checked my watch. Almost five. I was getting hungry and I had a date tonight. I adjusted the mic on my headset and spoke up. "Barry, this is what I want you to do. Unbuckle yourself and climb back here. We're switching seats."

Barry was an organizer of the local biking club and might have weighed one-thirty soaking wet. I could fly the plane from either side, but getting hefty ol' Keith out of that cockpit and squeezed back into the passenger seats would have taken a winch and a fifty-five gallon drum of vaseline.

Keith manned the controls while Barry and I switched seats, Barry chose the inelegant method of climbing head-first through the gap between the seats and it ended with him crawling on hands and knees to get upright again. I took the return path with my left foot forward so as to avoid some of the awkwardness.

Once I was settled in the pilot's seat, I assessed the situation. We were on an extended downwind, several miles out from the airport. The tower knew about our issue from our previous fly-bys and Marcy's voice came over the radio again shortly after I'd donned Barry's unpleasantly damp headset.

"November four five eight echo tango, say intentions."

I keyed the microphone in the yoke. "Hey, Marcy, it's Luke. I'm up here with these guys and I've got an idea for landing this Seneca, but it might jam up one of your runways. You have a preference on which one I put out of commission?"

"Big priority is getting you boys down safely. Wind is zero three zero at four knots. You can have runway seven or three-six."

Runway seven faced the prevailing winds more frequently. It would be a pain to have to close it, but if what I had in mind went well, it wouldn't be for long. The north-south runway was shorter, and with the water of Tampa Bay off both ends, it was considerably less forgiving.

"I'll continue for runway seven," I said. "And I'll try to land it short of runway three-six so I don't bugger up your whole evening."

Marcy's voice took on a serious note. "You want fire and rescue?"

I glanced over at Keith in the copilot seat. "I don't think that'll be necessary. I plan to have this thing on the ground in three minutes, so they'd be missing the show anyway."

"All right. Your call. Be safe."

I double-clicked the mic button to acknowledge her transmission and focused on the next step.

"What are you planning to do?" Keith asked, his fingers still white-knuckled on the yoke.

"You ever belly land a plane before?"

His face blanched. "You want to come in gear up?"

"No other options. We try to land with only the right main and the nose wheel down, we'll cartwheel this thing down the runway in a fireball."

"But hey now, the props . . . the doggone engines. The overhaul costs . . . my plane's going to be a total loss."

"You value your plane more than your life, Keith? That's what insurance is for."

"Sure. But . . . hell."

"Don't worry. I have an idea about your engines. My controls?"

He held on one last moment, then relinquished his grip. "Your controls."

Finally.

I slipped my lucky aviator sunglasses from the neck of my shirt and put them on, then watched the horizon as I raised the landing gear. The two green landing gear lights blinked out and the plane picked up speed.

I keyed the mic. "Albert Whitted Tower, November four five eight echo tango is turning right base for runway seven."

Marcy came back immediately. "Eight echo tango, you are cleared to land on runway seven."

"Not to be forward, Marcy, but I'd appreciate if you could have a good look at my undercarriage as we come around on final, make sure those landing gear are really stowed."

I could detect the smile in Marcy's voice as she came back on. "You use that line on all the tower controllers?"

"Dave and Jim don't seem to enjoy it as much when they're on duty." I brought the plane around the right turn and lined up for the runway.

"Had to get my binoculars out to see it, Luke, but your undercarriage is looking fine. Oh hang on. I do see what looks like a left gear door partially down, but your wheels are up."

"Thanks, Marcy, and I'll forgive the binoculars comment. Gets chilly in the wind, you know."

I kept the airspeed up on the final approach.

"Aren't you coming in a little hot?" Keith asked from the passenger seat. "I usually approach at ninety knots."

"Yeah, but I don't want to be short on airspeed. Not going to use flaps until I have to. We'll only get one shot at this with the engines off." I reached for the control column and pulled both throttles and the fuel mixture controls.

"With the WHAT off?" Keith's voice went up an octave as both engines sputtered and quit.

"Don't worry. Better this way."

The altimeter read four hundred feet.

I kept the plane steady and eyed the runway centerline. With the engines shut down, I had to pitch lower to keep our speed up. I shoved the throttles forward again to stop the warning horns from buzzing, then relished the ensuing quiet. We were a heavy-ass glider now, and coming down fast.

"You sure this is a good idea, Luke?" Barry squeaked from the back. I could tell he was still sweating just from his voice. We were going to need a dehumidifier soon.

"Regs say you only have to overhaul the engines if there's sudden stoppage, right?" I reached for the starter switches and bumped each of them a couple times. This was the key step. The two-bladed propellers had stopped in an angled downward position, but with a little nudging from the starters, they leveled out horizontally, and theoretically out of harm's way. "Get your seatbelts tight, boys."

"Gawd, I hope you're right about this," Keith muttered as the ground came up to meet us. He reached for the overhead door handle and popped it loose just in case we went in hard and crumpled our exit route. As the painted runway numbers vanished beneath us, I put both of my hands on the control yoke and pulled back, flaring the nose and bleeding off airspeed.

"'I've always said it's best to pretend like you're never going to land, just float down the runway two feet off the ground." My voice strained slightly from the effort to keep the plane in the right attitude.

But we didn't stay up long. Gravity always wins.

The damaged gear door hit first and instantly departed the plane.

The impact of the rest of the aircraft eliminated any chance of comment from my passengers. Aluminum meeting concrete at eighty miles per hour is deafening. I kept my grip on the yoke, even though there was no controlling the plane now. We were a projectile more than a vehicle. I clenched my jaw and hung on. Sparks flew from something. Tailpipes maybe. But as we ground along the asphalt, it was evident that as projectiles go, we were at least staying more of a frisbee than a bowling ball.

The plane finally ground to a stop.

Keith lifted his head from the cringing crash position he'd assumed.

We were only a few feet off the runway centerline. Nothing was even on fire. But we got the hell out of the plane in a hurry anyway.

When we gathered on the grass between the runway and the neighboring taxiway, Keith had his hand on his heart, but it was relief and not the coronary. We were alive, and as far as damage from forced landings go, this was going to be minor. I squatted and assessed the underside of the plane. With a little sheet metal work and the obvious landing gear adjustment, it might be back in the sky in a few weeks.

When I stood again, Barry slapped me on the back, a wide grin on his face. "That was the wildest thing I've ever seen, Luke. The way you thought to move the props out of the way and save the engines. Amazing. I can't get over it." He turned to Keith. "Told you he was the best in the business."

"Got lucky. I'm sure you boys could've done the same thing."

"Like hell," Keith said. "Never would have thought of that,

and I've owned a dozen airplanes. I don't know how you stayed so calm."

I felt like mentioning that no one had even been shooting at us in this scenario. I'd certainly been through worse. But I let him ramble his gratitude a while longer. The near-death experience, plus me saving him a fortune, had him flying high again.

A few looky-loos had made it out to the runway in golf carts. I spotted one member of my own maintenance crew and gave her a nod. Reese, my best mechanic, had already thought to bring the jacks. With any luck we'd have the plane off the runway in short order.

I checked my watch again. Looked like there was only one downside to this situation.

I was going to be late for my date.

TWO
MISSING PIECE

REESE WINTER and I only crossed paths for one tour in the Army, the end of my career and the beginning of hers, but it had been memorable. She was the only female intel officer I'd worked with who had been attached to a sniper unit. But her gender wasn't what made her a standout. Keeping cool under fire tests a person's mettle, and working together under fire tests a relationship like nothing else.

Reese's convoy had been decimated by RPGs in an ambush while returning from a remote surveillance outpost. I'd been the one to go get them. Things went from shit to FUBAR. Some days leave a mark, and when you land a UH-60 full of dead and wounded while your fellow soldier keeps pressure on a bullet wound in your neck, your friendship welds like titanium.

So now we'd have each other's backs till Kingdom Come.

That's why when I got out of the Army, I'd told her to come find me when she was done. A few years later she did.

She stood out here, same as she always had, but having her in my life again was a puzzle piece I'd been missing, and it settled something in my soul. Turned out her analytical mind also made her one hell of a mechanic. Plus my dog loved her, and he was a better judge of character than anyone.

Murphy had ridden out on the golf cart too and hadn't waited for it to come to a complete stop before running over to greet me. I got a brief happy bump in the knees from his muscled shoulders, then a furtive lick of my hand before he was off again, sniffing the others and doing a lap of the plane. I'd never let him on an active runway any other day so he was going to capitalize on this rare opportunity to pee on fresh turf.

Reese must have been listening to the radio during my landing of the Seneca because she'd come out to the runway prepared.

"You want to get jacking?" she asked. "Or do we need to wait for the feds?"

"The FAA will send somebody to have a look, but they won't mind if we drag it off the runway first."

Plenty of people were milling around, a couple of flight students with their instructors, and several line guys from the FBO. Howard, our aging fuel truck driver, had parked nearby and was leaning out the driver's window watching.

I left it to Keith and Barry to describe what had happened to the curious onlookers and the two of them enjoyed the spotlight.

I only paused to fire off one text.

>>> Stuck working late. Could still do drinks. Want to meet me at eight? Irish place on Beach Drive?

The reply came immediately.

<<< See you there.

I smiled. Then Reese and I focused on getting to work.

It took the better part of an hour.

Eventually, the plane was jacked, the landing gear brought down, and the plane towed off the runway. We didn't take it far. My hangar was full at the moment so we left it on a tie down on the nearby taxiway, but we'd get to it in the morning. Keith and

Barry gave me one more round of appreciative handshakes before I was free to climb on the golf cart with Reese and Murphy and make our way back to the hangar.

I exhaled a sigh of relief getting free of the crowd around the plane. I wouldn't be able to avoid attention over the next few days, especially once the story circulated, but since it was the end of the day, I'd at least get some peace for the night.

That was the plan anyway.

But as Reese and Murph and I rolled back to the comforting sight of Hangar 4, it wasn't as vacant as I liked. A pair of uniformed Saint Petersburg police officers were lingering around the Cessna 206 floatplane I had parked inside.

"You expecting the cops?" Reese asked.

"Hadn't been till now." The officers were a man and a woman. If the guy hadn't ever played college football it was a waste because he was built for it. The woman was fit as well, trim waist with generous hips and a uniform that was snug in flattering places.

I waited till Reese had pulled the golf cart into the hangar and drifted to a stop before hopping off. The officers lingering by the float plane looked on with neutral expressions. Murphy headed over to investigate them, and they gave my dog friendly pats as he sniffed their shoes. The guy was standing behind the woman and I had the impression she was in charge. I was proven right when I wandered their way and she was the first to speak. "Hi. We're looking for a Mr. Angel. Is that you?"

"Luke is fine. What's up?"

She glanced over my shoulder at Reese. "I'm Officer Hart and this is Officer Burns. We have a few questions we'd like to ask you. Is there somewhere we can talk?"

"Hart and Burns? Must get a lot of antacid jokes."

"You wouldn't be the first."

"Anything serious?"

"Serious enough to speak privately."

I gestured toward the stairs at the back corner. They led to the office overlooking the hangar floor. "We can shoot the breeze in peace up there."

"I like the sculpture," Hart said. "You make that?" She was referencing the sign that hung on the office wall. It was made of turbine blades, wrenches, gears and a few other gadgets welded together to form two expanded angel wings. It stretched eight feet. The welded cutouts across the central spar read "ARCHANGEL AVIATION."

"I hung that the day I signed the lease on this hangar. Good luck to whoever tries to take it down."

"You get that flag from a baseball stadium infield?" Officer Burns asked, referencing the American flag that hung below the welded wings. It was roughly the size of a tractor trailer.

"Just in case anyone forgets which country we're in," I said. "Some people are visual learners."

That flag and I had a lot of history, but not the kind I got gabby about. I led the way upstairs instead.

My office was small but tidy and boasted a sliver of water view out the window. The window faced the sunrise and admiring it over this inlet of Tampa Bay made mornings easier. The US Coast Guard station blocked much of the view, but I figured they were entitled to it. I got plenty of good views from higher altitudes.

There were exactly enough chairs for officers Hart and Burns so I invited them to sit and they did, adjusting their bulky gun belts to fit in the seats.

Murphy had likewise clambered his way up the stairs and did a couple of turns on his dog bed before plopping down to supervise the proceedings.

"Good-looking dog," Burns said. "What breed is he?"

"Brown dog with a little bit of white dog, far as I can tell."

Burns grunted his approval and folded his hands in his lap.

Officer Hart focused her gaze on me. "Mr. Angel, the reason we're here today is we have some questions about a client of yours, Dr. Christopher Carter."

"Chris? Sure. What's going on with him?"

"He's missing, Mr. Angel. And his wife believes you were the last person to see him."

THREE

CARTER

MY MIND REWOUND, reviewing the last twenty-four hours. Front and center was Chris Carter. In my office last night. Alive, present. No sign of trouble. Just another airplane conversation in a friendship that went back a decade. It took me a moment to realize Officer Hart had asked another question.

"Mr. Angel?"

"Sorry," I said. "Say it again?"

"Your relationship with Dr. Carter was more than business, is that correct? You were family?"

I rubbed my neck. "Used to be. I was married to his wife's sister, Cassidy, for a while."

"And were you close with Dr. Carter during that time?"

My hangar cat, Blackjack, chose that moment to climb out of my lower desk drawer and hop up into my lap. She stretched and arched her back. I rested a hand on her head as she purred. "Yeah. We used to be close. I was in his wedding. Cassidy and I are godparents to Chris and Ava's daughter, Harper. Haven't seen as much of him since my divorce. Mostly here at the airport. But we're still friends."

"Mrs. Carter told us you take care of Dr. Carter's plane and you would have access to his personal hangar. Is that the case?"

"I have a key."

"Mrs. Carter couldn't find one and we are hoping to establish the whereabouts of Dr. Carter's vehicle. Is it likely he put it in the hangar?"

"If he took the plane out, sure."

"Would you mind taking us there?"

"Happy to. Now?"

"In a few minutes. Could you tell us the last time you saw Dr. Carter?"

Officer Burns had a notepad out and a cheap blue Bic pen. He was having trouble with it. I plucked a pen from an old tin can at the edge of my desk and offered it to him. Burns grunted what might have been a thank you and took the pen.

"Chris stopped by to pick up his logbooks before I closed up shop yesterday. I keep them here since I do most of the work on his plane. Easier to keep track of maintenance entries that way. Said he wanted to make copies of a few things, something about renewing his insurance and needing the records."

"Is that a common occurrence?"

"Needing the records? Sometimes. Insurance likes to know how many hours you are putting on the plane every year and I don't think Chris is great at logging his flight hours. We all get lazy about it sometimes."

"What time was this?"

"I was working late. Maybe eight."

"Did he mention anything about taking a trip? Going out of town?"

"Not to me."

"Did Dr. Carter have a girlfriend?"

Detective Hart made good eye contact. Not oppressive, but direct. She had stellar eye lashes even with minimal make-up.

Not bad to look at, though I imagined doing police work wasn't the peak of her attention to fashion. Her jaw set tightly when she wasn't speaking, but I could tell she was actively attempting to keep her posture from appearing too rigid. Trying to keep me relaxed most likely. It was easy to see why she was in charge.

"Not that I'm aware of. Good father. Adored his wife. Maybe too much."

"You don't have a high opinion of Mrs. Carter?"

"She can be a challenging personality. When Cassidy and I got divorced, I tried to steer clear of Ava. You've met her?"

It was Burns who nodded, eyes widening slightly.

Hart gave him a sideways glance.

"What? She's memorable," Burns said.

"Well put together. Perks of being married to a plastic surgeon," I said. "But she and I don't mix."

"Was Dr. Carter aware of your dislike of his wife?" Hart asked.

"Didn't say I didn't like her. I just avoid her."

"Some might say that's the same thing."

"It's not."

Hart tucked her tongue into her cheek while she assessed me, then went on with her questioning.

"Any reason someone at the airport would have an issue with Dr. Carter?"

"Gets along fine with everyone as far as I know. He has a tendency to be a bit of a people pleaser usually. You're sure he and Ava didn't just have a fight and he took a trip to cool off?"

"We're considering all possibilities at the moment. Any racial, political, or religious tensions in his life that you are aware of?"

"Chris got married in a church, but he's not super religious. Not sure where he leans politically. We don't get into it much. Mostly stick to planes or sports."

"Was Dr. Carter driving his own vehicle when you saw him?"

"Don't know. Might have been parked farther down. We had a lot of planes tied out front cluttering things up last night. We run out of space in the hangar quickly when we get busy."

Hart glanced around the office. "You make your living primarily from maintenance?"

I shifted in my seat. "Among other things. We've got a charter certificate, float plane tours, a little aerial photography work. There's always plenty to keep us busy." Blackjack decided to climb my chest and was attempting to rub her head on the stubble of my chin. I hoisted her onto the desk to get her out of my face and she flicked her tail in annoyance.

"Got a lot of animals around here," Officer Burns said. I guess he was in charge of making all the obvious statements.

"In a big airplane hangar, you can have a cat, or you can have rats. Most people prefer this option."

I turned to Officer Hart and hooked a thumb toward the door. "Want to go see the hangar now?"

"I do."

I snatched the key to Chris's hangar from inside my file cabinet and led the way down the stairs again. Murphy came too.

Reese was still lingering on the hangar floor, though it looked like most of the tools had been cleaned up.

"Everything good?" she asked, her eyes drifting to the cops behind me.

"Yeah. I'll fill you in later." I twirled the hangar key ring around my index finger gunslinger-style. "We'll have a busy few days if we end up with that Seneca work."

"I'll come in early. Barry stopped by a minute ago. Sounds like he's still interested in the plane if we can fix it."

"My landing probably brought the price down for him."

"Could have gone the other way," she argued. "Bet half the airport has heard about your landing by now."

"I'll catch Barry tomorrow. Need to go help these two with something else."

Reese nodded but didn't pry.

Officers Hart and Burns were waiting near the main hangar door. I joined them and gestured toward the golf cart. "This is our ride."

Hart took the front, while Burns eased his considerable bulk onto the rear-facing seat on the back. Murphy wriggled his way in front of Hart on the floor and sat on her feet. We rolled out onto the taxiway. The Carters had a hangar at the east end of the field and it was a short ride by golf cart. I pulled up out front and fished the key from my pocket.

"If you don't mind, we'll enter first," Detective Hart said. She'd donned gloves.

I handed her the key. "Be my guest. Murph, stay." The dog sat.

Maybe it was habit, but Hart had a hand resting on her gun when she pushed the door open.

"Light switch is on the left," I said.

She found it. The overhead fluorescent bulbs shed a weak light but were better than nothing.

Burns followed his partner through the door and I caught it before it closed, stepping over the threshold but staying near the door.

The hangar smelled strongly of avgas.

Chris's red-and-white Cessna 210 was gone and his black Mercedes coupe sat in its place. The hangar had some of the usual clutter they acquired, a few cast off bits of patio furniture, a stand up paddle board, and several boxes of Chris's college junk Ava must have jettisoned from the house. Chris had a tool box and a metal shelf stacked with the usual pilot bric-a-brac of old airport directories and cans of windshield cleaner. Officers Hart and Burns circled the Mercedes with flashlights. The car was vacant. Hart tried the door handle and found it unlocked.

I had my hands in my pockets, but my eyes roamed and immediately alit on the one thing out of place in the hangar. On a shelf above the tool box, next to an old picture of Harper, sat Chris's wallet and phone.

"Guys," I said, and pointed to the shelf. Hart got there first. Her flashlight glinted off the phone screen and her expression darkened. She opened the wallet enough to check the ID. I didn't need to see it to know it belonged to Chris. And I recognized that if you flew off into the sunset without your wallet and phone, there's a good chance you weren't headed anywhere good.

FOUR

DREAD

"WE'D APPRECIATE it if you could keep all of this to yourself as much as possible until we know more," Officer Hart said. "We're going to call this report in to our sergeant and will likely get the detective bureau involved. They may have some more questions for you."

We were back in front of my hangar again, after a somber ride back. Murphy was the only one unaffected by the mood. He lay near the officers with his forepaws crossed, panting happily with his eyes on me.

"Seems like you're treating this as a crime," I said.

"Until we know more about where Dr. Carter departed to."

"I might be able to help with that." I took out my phone and checked Flight Aware. The website tracked most flights. I entered in the Cessna 210's registration number. Sure enough, a portion of a flight showed from last night, but the track was headed out to the gulf. It ended over open water.

Damn. Maybe it had lost contact for some reason. Tech glitches happened. But that didn't satisfy the knot in my gut.

There was nothing much out that way, just open water all the way to Mexico.

I took a screen shot, then handed my phone to Officer Hart.

"How accurate is this site?"

"Pretty reliable," I acknowledged. "You going to call the Coast Guard?"

"Once this is handed off to our sergeant, he'll take it from there, but you can be sure search and rescue will be notified. How did you come up with this image?"

I told them and Officer Burns took notes.

"If you can stick around, it might be useful," Hart said.

I checked my watch. "Supposed to be meeting someone in a few minutes, what happens if I don't stay?"

Hart and Burns exchanged glances.

"Not going far, 'bout a half mile that way. On foot."

"Keep your phone on. Don't stray too far in the next few hours if you don't mind."

It occurred to me that I could hop in my plane and fly over the gulf right now, see if I could find Chris. But it was getting dark, and search and rescue didn't need me in the way right from the get go.

"You'll talk to Ava now, I suspect."

Hart nodded. "We'll let her know what we've found. I'd encourage you not to jump to any conclusions until we know more. This is an active investigation and we appreciate your discretion."

They were drawing conclusions of their own and we both knew it.

"Where will you be if we need you?" Officer Burns asked.

"Irish bar down the street. Or at the marina."

"I'll hold you to that."

Murphy and I lingered while they walked back toward Chris's hangar.

Then I closed my hangar door and sighed.

Shit, Chris. What the hell were you thinking?

For a guy set on flying off to the great beyond, he hadn't seemed agitated when I'd seen him. But we weren't exactly close anymore. He was unlikely to confide in me. Ava had made it pretty clear I wasn't in her family anymore, so whatever Chris was up to, I doubt she wanted me meddling. The professionals were already on it.

Besides, I'd rescued enough people for one day.

I checked my watch.

I was going to be late. Again.

My headspace wasn't in a place for romance, but my date tonight had already changed plans once and I'd hate to reward her perseverance by bailing on her twice. Plus we'd been set up by Marcy, and I knew better than to ignore instructions from my favorite tower controller. My date was probably circling the pub looking for parking right now, and if I knew anything about women, there was an hour of prep she'd pulled off to get there.

Meant I couldn't roll up smelling like motor oil and Barry's ear sweat.

In the back corner near the makeshift kitchen was the hangar's only restroom and I'd installed a shower in it. Occasionally it came in handy, like the time one of my mechanics had inadvertently drenched himself in avgas defueling a plane. Tonight it was more standard use. I stripped naked and climbed in, determined to be quick, but it was hard to keep my mind from wandering back to Chris's empty hangar and that ominous flight track. We'd had a plane go missing once before that way. Guy flew off into the night and never came back. It was rare, but it happened. Even pilots get depressed sometimes.

But Chris? Doctor with a beautiful wife, great kid. It had to be a simpler explanation. People forget their phones sometimes. He was probably fine.

Maybe.

I climbed out of the shower smelling like Ivory bar soap and cheap hotel shampoo, but it was better than I'd smelled before.

There was a Rubbermaid cabinet in the bathroom where I kept a change of clothes: fresh jeans and a linen shirt with a socially acceptable amount of wrinkles. Flip flops and a mussing of my hair finished the look. It would have to do. I hadn't shaved in a few days but stubble was in, right? Plus it did a decent job of covering my scar.

Murphy was waiting for me by the hangar door. I snatched his leash from a hook and stuffed it into my back pocket before locking up.

The runway lights were lit while we hiked across the tarmac and past the flight school. A few stars were out and the neighboring skyline of towering condos decorated the horizon to the north. A pair of lights in the sky to the west looked a bit like stars till they got closer, revealing themselves as the landing lights of an incoming Beechcraft King Air.

Murphy and I took the track behind the runway 7 blast fence. The shortcut would save time and got us the prime view of the King Air as it blasted in forty feet over our heads. That view never got old.

The King Air's tires chirped to the runway beyond us and the reversing propellers on the twin PT6 engines redirected the thrust with a roar.

The tower lights were still on, but Marcy would be quitting soon. Then this place would go back to being an uncontrolled airport for the night.

According to Flight Aware, this was around the same time last night that Chris would have been prepping for departure. Had Marcy seen him take off?

The Hangar Restaurant and Flight Lounge was teeming with patrons as I cruised out the pedestrian gate to the street. There was a more direct route to the pub I was headed to, but I couldn't resist taking the slightly longer waterside path. The sidewalk wrapped around the Dali Museum and hugged the marina with a view of the St. Pete Pier.

The city was alive and bustling at this hour. A gaggle of runners passed me, lit up with glowing arm bands and reflective athletic wear. Most of them were women and I appreciated the scenery as they cruised by. God bless whoever invented lycra and lululemon.

The pub was busy when I showed up. Murphy did the rounds greeting the regulars at the outside tables. I received a few nods too, but it was no secret who the popular one was. I went inside and kept my eyes open. Plenty of familiar faces, and one solo act drawing attention. Her long brown legs were bare all the way to the stool she was on, the black, split-hem tube dress arresting focus from there. She'd covered her shoulders with a thin sweater and had her purse in her lap as she conversed with Danielle, one of the bartenders. Her dark hair fell over one shoulder and partially obscured her features, but gold peeked through from her earrings. I did a quick scan of the rest of the bar to verify my suspicion, then walked over.

Danielle spotted me first and lifted her chin.

Marie pivoted on her stool and her eyes widened, smiling.

"Hi, Marie. Better late than never, right?"

"I'd almost decided to go home with Danni here. Turns out she knows all my favorite drinks."

"Wise choice. Hey, Danni. Thanks for keeping her company for me."

"Had to give her a sanity test for going on a date with you."

"Did she pass?"

"She's still here so she has to be bonkers."

Marie set her purse on the bar and shrugged out of her sweater as I sat, exposing her bare shoulders and the rest of the outfit she'd been hiding. Or lack of outfit as it turned out. The upper half of the dress allowed a generous view of skin. I'd seen a picture of her before—thanks to Marcy. Even exchanged a few flirty messages, but the real-life Marie was better-than-advertised. She brushed her hair away from her face and smiled. "Everybody knows you around here."

"Don't believe anything they tell you. Herd of liars."

"Guy over there named Leroy says 'you practically live here' and 'he taught you everything you know about darts.'"

"Hmm."

"Danielle spoke highly of you, says you're a great tipper. But apparently your dog is nicer than you are."

"Facts."

"I told her I'd have to be the one to judge that. She also said you live on a boat."

"That's temporarily true."

"Sounds charming."

"As long as you don't get seasick."

"Is it a nice boat?"

"Nicer than I deserve. You hungry?"

"I had something when you said you'd be late. But I'll keep you company if you want to order."

"I'll settle for liquid dinner." Despite my reassurances to myself, I found the news about Chris had robbed me of an appetite.

Marie reached into her purse. "Okay, then first round's on me." She slapped her credit card on the bar.

"Never. I kept you waiting, least I can do is buy." I reached for my wallet.

"First thing to know about me, I went to law school specifically so I'd win all my arguments in bars." She passed her card across to Danielle. "Another dirty martini for me, and I'm betting you know his usual."

Danielle took the card and gave me another raised eyebrow.

"The lady wins all her arguments," I said.

Marie smiled. "I like a man who can follow a plan."

"We have a plan?"

"Of course we do. I'm going to get a couple of drinks in you and you're going to show me your pretty boat."

Turns out I liked a woman with a plan.

FIVE
FEELING DATED

THE MOON REFLECTED off the water at Demens Landing. By the time Marie and I made our way to the marina, the stars were bright and night had cooled. Marie shivered as we walked through the gate to the boat slips, but instead of donning the sweater slung over her bag, she opted to lean into me instead.

I put an arm around her bare shoulder and we steadied ourselves on the narrow walkway. Our hours at the bar had been full of easy laughter and a strong dose of chemistry. I liked her. We'd found something comfortable in each other's company and she was easy to be around. I hadn't had a date go this well in a long time, and while I hadn't been specifically looking for one, Marie had serious girlfriend potential.

The physical contact had started early, her hand grazing mine in conversation, her bare knees nudging mine from the neighboring barstool. She slid an arm around me now as we passed a forest of sailboat masts and a half dozen sizable motor yachts before reaching the final slip.

The fifty-three foot catamaran took up the entire end of the dock and nearly glowed in the moonlight.

"Whoa," Marie said as we approached.

The yacht was a looker. It's twin hulls rode high and even with its sails stowed, it looked fast. And fun. Marie's eyes roamed over the boat appreciatively until she spotted the name placard affixed to it. She looked to me. "*Hank's Midlife Crisis?*"

"I have a confession to make."

She gave me a quizzical stare from beneath her long lashes.

"I said I live on a boat. I never said it was *my* boat."

"Thought maybe you had an alias."

"Hank's a friend of mine. Lives up in the condos above the bar we were just in. Known him for a long time and I look after his boat for him."

"That's a good friend. Was he at that bar tonight? Maybe I chose the wrong date."

"Can't argue your questionable taste in men, but Hank's off the market. Has been for fifty years."

"Fifty?"

"Younger woman too. His wife is only seventy. Hank is eighty-five. Married her when he was in his thirties and she was twenty."

"Wow. *Midlife Crisis?*"

"Bought it last year. He's a raging optimist."

Marie laughed. "Sounds like quite the guy."

"One of the best men I know."

"Permission to come aboard, captain?"

Murphy rushed across the gangplank first, then I took Marie's hand and helped her across to the stern deck.

It was a fancy yacht. I hadn't been lying when I said it was nicer than I deserved. I spent a fair amount of time wiping up the messy fingerprints I made coming home from working in the hangar. Thankfully, even expensive yacht furnishings are made to be scrubbed.

I unlocked the sliding glass door from the stern deck to the main living area of the boat and Marie entered first. It was cozy but well-appointed, with an L-shaped couch catercorner to the kitchen and a third corner housing a navigation console that could be mistaken for the desk in a luxury office. The skylights let in some of the glow from the city skyline until I flipped on the galley lights and dimmed them.

Marie let out a sigh. "I can see how you'd get used to this."

There was a hook to my left for Murphy's leash so I hung that and made my way to the kitchen cabinets. "Pretty sure I've got martini glasses in here somewhere. You want another?"

"Hmm. I'm right in that happy place where fun still has dignity. Another might make me sloppy."

She had set her purse on the coffee table and slipped off her sandals, then followed me toward the galley. It was a cozy space, not a lot of room to maneuver. She brushed some hair behind her ear but kept her eyes on mine. A collision seemed imminent. The lighting was dim, and she had a lot of curves to run aground on.

She had me cornered but I didn't mind. She reached out and pressed her hands to my stomach, then ran them up my chest. My sunglasses still hung from the collar of my shirt and she pulled them loose.

"Careful with those. Those are my lucky shades."

"Lucky, huh? Then I definitely want them." She placed them on her head and smirked. "How lucky will I get now?"

"Interesting question." I wrapped one hand around the curve of her hip and then let it glide to the small of her back. She eased into me slow, then ran her hands over my shoulders.

"You get all these muscles flying planes? Didn't think you had to flap your arms to make them stay up."

"Who said I fly? I'm just a lowly grease monkey."

"Marcy says. Plus, I googled you."

"Oh, did you now."

"Luke Angel, decorated combat veteran. Owner of

Archangel Aviation. You'd be surprised at what us lawyers can dig up." She was grinding her hips into mine, adhering herself to me, and it felt great. She slung her arms around my neck and played with my hair. "A girl has to do her research somehow, but I do need to file a complaint about your lack of social media presence. Luke Angel's personal life is an online enigma."

"That's not a plus?" I put my other hand around her back, stroking the edges of her spine with my fingertips. "You couldn't have dug up all my secrets. You're still here."

Her lips were only inches from mine now and her perfume smelled damned good.

"It *is* difficult to stalk you when the only web page you own is just pictures of airplanes."

"Good-looking airplanes."

"I'm more interested in the man behind the machines." Her lips grazed mine, then lingered just out of reach. Tantalizing. We could cat and mouse this a while longer, but we both knew where things were headed. I took the bait and plunged, taking her mouth with mine and pulling her the rest of the way to me. Her breath caught as I pressed her to me, her full breasts smashed against my chest.

Her kisses were warm and alternated between coy and hungry.

She kept her mouth on mine as she lifted one leg, running her bare foot up the side of my calf. The movement caused the hem of her already short dress to ride up her thigh. I ran my hand down the leg as far as her knee, then back up again. The edge of her dress retreated even farther this time till I felt the thin fabric of her panties at her hip.

She whispered in my ear. "I don't think I need those anymore."

Her willingness to shed clothes was faster than I usually moved on a first date, but I lacked a good reason to argue.

I hooked my thumbs over the edges of her panties and pulled them off her hips. She wriggled till they dropped to the floor.

Marie had her fingers in my hair again. I cupped her butt and lifted her onto the kitchen island, then she wrapped both legs around me. Her kisses slowed but deepened, her tongue playing with mine. She only paused to unbutton my shirt. "If I lose clothes, you do too. Fair is fair."

"I'm starting to understand how you win all your arguments. You're very persuasive."

My shirt ended up on the floor with her underwear.

"It's a nice kitchen," she mumbled through a kiss, "but does this boat come with beds?"

"Downstairs. Seems far."

"Feels weird to take the rest of my clothes off with your dog watching. He and I just met."

I glanced over to find Murphy following our activity from the couch.

"You just met me too."

"Yeah, but I like you. A lot."

"Hmm." Words were difficult with our mouths so busy. Mine found its way down her neck to the top of her chest.

"You need to take a break to google *me* a little?"

"Not the activity I had in mind."

My hands were stroking the outsides of her thighs, but she took one of them and moved it between her legs. I obliged. She moaned, then gasped in my ear. "Okay. Which stairs to the bed?"

"Starboard."

"It's stupid that saying it in a boaty way makes it sexier."

"Want me to say more boat stuff? Thruster. Head. Drive shaft."

She giggled.

"Poop deck?"

"Nope. Now you're ruining it."

"No poop deck stuff. Got it."

I scooped her up and carried her the few feet to the starboard hull stairs. There was no way to gracefully traverse it together, so I let her slide down me till her feet touched the floor.

"Bottom of the stairs and aft. The end with the bed in it."

She let one hand trail down my chest and then over the front of my pants. She grinned and tugged my zipper open before she vanished down the stairs. I took a deep breath, then followed. Reaching the bottom, my foot found the immaterial excuse for a dress she'd been wearing.

The lights weren't on in this cabin, but I had a suspicion we wouldn't need them for anything Marie had in mind. I found my way to her through the dark just fine.

SIX
CASSIDY

THE ALARM on my phone was set for six, but I was out of bed at a quarter till. The first hints of daylight appeared in the sky to the east while I had the coffee brewing. The morning quiet was only broken by the crunching noises coming from Murphy at his food bowl.

Marie was still asleep in my bed, so I took my coffee and a notepad outside and climbed up to the bow of the boat. I had a deck chair there that made for a good spot to think, and that's what I needed.

I closed my eyes, homing in on the gentle rise and fall of the boat and the creaking sounds the craft made in the breeze. The scent of the coffee amid the tang of salt air was almost enough to convince me I was having a normal day. But as water lapped the sides of the catamaran, it made me think of the gulf and the dead end track of Chris's plane on Flight Aware. I had the image of his Cessna 210 floating in open water, then slowly sinking beneath the waves. I tried to reconcile what I knew of the man with the idea of him ending it all at sea. It didn't make sense.

By the time my coffee mug was halfway empty, the clouds on

the distant horizon were pink. The morning sky was mostly clear with a scattered layer up around five-thousand feet. Good visibility.

The somber tone of Officer Hart's voice when I'd left the airport told me she wasn't hopeful. I was sure they'd notified search and rescue. The Coast Guard was probably out there right now. Even if suicide was suspected, they'd go search. But the question rattling around my head was whether or not I knew more about Chris's character than the facts suggested. Could there be some other reason he flew out over the gulf? Was there a chance he was anywhere other than dead in the water right now?

I mulled it over and decided that whatever the investigation and search turned up, it wouldn't hurt to look into it myself. Chris and I weren't the best of friends lately, but he'd been family once, and I wasn't going to let him go without doing at least something to help. When the sun came up, I'd go up too.

I'd already worked through which plane to take and a general plan of attack, but my train of thought was interrupted by the sound of footsteps on the dock. They were getting closer. I pivoted in my deck chair and spotted the slender figure approaching the boat. She was wearing her airline uniform this morning, minus the hat and jacket, and I recognized the walk as her most business-like, the brisk, efficient strides of a woman who knows what she wants. I hadn't seen it lately, but that was because for the past few years, she hadn't wanted me to.

Cassidy Angel stood about five-seven in flats, tan and athletic as the day we married. She'd been blessed with the genes for delicate features and slender hands—hands unencumbered by the sparkling rings I'd once given her. Today her honey-brown hair was pulled up in a ponytail and she had her collar unbuttoned to a depth that wasn't regulation. She'd lost the tie but still wore her captain's epaulets. I knew this was one of her just-got-off-work outfits, but she still looked damned good in it.

Murphy sprinted down the gangplank and was at her feet in a flash, his entire butt wiggling with the effort of wagging his tail.

"Hey, Murph," she said, unable to resist his attention. She squatted to scratch his chest with her nails the way he liked, then her eyes finally met mine. She stood back to her full height. "Hello, Luke."

I did still like the way she said my name. She always put a little sex in it.

"Look who's back in town." I climbed out of my deck chair and leaned on the railing.

She appraised me from a distance. "You look the same."

I glanced down at my bare chest and board shorts. "Didn't know you were coming. I might've put on a shirt."

"Since when did that ever happen?" There was a hint of the old playfulness in her voice, but then her expression darkened. "You heard about Chris?"

"Police came by the airport last night. You just get in?"

"Took a jump-seat on a red-eye as soon as I got back from my west coast trip."

"Shit situation. How's Ava?"

"Inconsolable."

"And Harper?"

Cassidy sighed. "Ava says she's confused and worried. But doing as okay as an eleven-year old can be in this situation."

"She's a tough kid. Hate that she's going through this." I gripped the bow rail tighter.

"They were still asleep when I went by and dropped my bag, so I thought I'd see if I could catch you before work."

"You caught me."

Cassidy took a few steps closer on the dock. "Okay, so one reason I came by . . . is that my dad is in town too, and he has this idea in his head—"

"Luke? I'm hoping this coffee is fair game?" The voice came

from inside, and a moment later, Marie appeared bearing a coffee mug and wearing one of my company T-shirts. It barely offered coverage beyond her upper thigh.

"Oh. Sorry," she blurted when she saw Cassidy. "Didn't realize you were talking to someone out here."

The two women only locked eyes for a second, but I had a feeling a lot was said in that look. Then Marie headed back inside. She gave me an apologetic grimace. "I'll leave you two alone."

Cassidy's gaze followed, tracking the young woman's rear end, and her eyes narrowed at the sight of the winged Archangel Aviation logo across the back of the shirt.

"I see you've been making some *new* angels," she said. And any warmth in her voice was gone.

"Wasn't expecting you."

"No problem. I'll leave you to your guest."

"You were saying something about your dad."

She hiked her purse up her shoulder. "You know what? It's nothing. I've got a lot to do with Ava and Harper, and I can see I'm intruding."

"Figuring out what happened to Chris takes priority."

"Clearly. Your friend is from search and rescue?"

"Don't be catty. Or maybe *Vince* can help with whatever you need."

Cassidy's eyes burned into mine, then she pivoted on her heel and strode away.

Shit. That hadn't been what I wanted to say at all.

I vaulted over the bow rail and landed on the dock. But Cassidy was already a good way down. "Cass! Stop."

But she didn't. She walked faster. She blew out the gate at the far end and by the time I'd jogged to the fence she was in her car. I tried to get her attention, but she pointedly ignored me. The tires of her rental left three feet of rubber exiting the parking lot.

I swore all my most colorful expletives on my walk back to the boat.

Real smooth, Luke.

When I made it back aboard the *Midlife Crisis,* I found Marie climbing the steps from the guest quarters to the kitchen. She was back in her dress and sweater from the night before and had her hair tied up in a bun. She cringed when she saw me. "Sorry, I hope I didn't embarrass you. Was that . . .?" She left the question hanging in mid air like a balloon ready to burst.

"My ex-wife," I said. "And don't worry about it. Not your problem."

"She's gone?"

"Something she's good at."

Marie gave me a sympathetic smile. "I'll get out of your hair too. Thanks for letting me sleep over. Last night was fun."

"No problem." I opened the sliding door for her.

She gave me a peck on the corner of my mouth. "You don't have to walk me out. I'll be fine. I'll call you, okay?"

"Sure."

She gave the dog one last pat on her way, then she was down the gangplank and out of sight. Murphy panted happily as he watched her go.

"Day's off to a banner start, huh, buddy?"

From his point of view, it probably was.

Some days were better spent as a dog.

SEVEN
DALE

I TOOK my old Jeep to the airport, and when I rolled up to Hangar 4, it was already open. Reese was busy moving planes around. She gave me a nod as I walked up, but her eyes flitted to the office.

"Just a heads up, you've got company."

"Not more cops, is it?"

"Figured you might have called an owner meeting. Looks like you're getting one."

A figure moved into view upstairs and I recognized the short silver hair and glasses.

"Shit. Dale's here?"

"Was hanging around when I showed up. He insisted on waiting in your office."

I grumbled as I made my way to the stairs.

Mornings were hard enough without people showing up ahead of shop hours. There was an order to how a day was supposed to flow and I liked it to start with a second cup of coffee and silence.

Exes were not part of my preferred morning routine and ex-father-in-laws ranked lowest on the chart of people I wanted to see.

Murphy followed me up the stairs and I opened the door to my office to find Dale Dobbs sitting in my swivel chair. He wore tan slacks and a burgundy golf polo. His loafers had tassels.

"Luke. About time."

The clock on the wall read 7:05.

"Shop opens at eight, Dale."

"You always let employees have free access?"

"Reese is welcome any hour."

"Newest employee, maybe you ought to have a probationary period before employees get keys."

"Tyson is actually our newest employee."

"He's that young black boy you hired."

"Hank Martin's grandson."

"Ah. Right. I suppose you give him a key too."

"Every employee gets a key, Dale. That what you're here for? I'll cut you one."

Dale leaned over and rubbed his fingers together, making a kissy sound to get Murphy's attention. "Come here, doggy."

Murphy considered him from a distance but didn't move.

"You don't train your dog to come?"

"You're in my chair, Dale. What can I do for you?"

He stopped trying to entice the dog and looked at me. "You know about the situation with Chris?"

"I'm in the loop."

"Goddamn nightmare. Ava's holding it together because she's a trooper, but it's a shit time. The cops said you were at the hangar so you must have seen?"

"I let the detectives in. Saw his wallet and phone, that's all I know. Did they launch search and rescue?"

"For all the good it will do them. He left a note on his phone. Depressed or some nonsense. Taking a four-hundred-thousand dollar airplane and plunking it in the Gulf as his exit. Cowardly move."

The anger in his voice took me aback. But he kept on.

"In my day, you worked through your issues. You didn't *abandon* your family and your problems and take the easy way out."

Hard to say which imaginary day in the past he was referring to when people didn't suffer from depression, but his red-faced fuming was just bluster. I'd let him vent. Wasn't hurting anyone here.

"I'm going to take the 206 out this morning," I said. "Follow the last track of the 210 and see what I can see."

"After more than thirty-six hours? You know that's a pipe dream, right? If the Coast Guard can't find him, what hope do you have?"

"I'm still going to look. Because I can."

"You've got a business to run. No one expects you to go flying around on search and rescue."

"Chris would."

Dale glowered at that but didn't argue. "I think your time would be best spent staying out of the way of the real search party. Or helping the people who didn't fly off into the sunset. But you do what you need to do."

I hadn't been asking permission, but he seemed to think I needed it.

"What can I do for you, Dale? You come to look at Chris's hangar too?"

Dale shifted in his seat. "No. Came for a different reason altogether. I've been talking to Ava and her mother and I think it might be a good idea if she and Harper come back to Boston for a bit, in light of the circumstances. And with Cassidy up there now too, there's not a lot keeping us tethered to Florida. Except this place." He gestured to the hangar.

I settled my hands on my hips. "You're thinking you want out of your thirty percent?"

"It's different circumstances now. When you and Cassidy were married it made sense. Her mother and I felt good about giving you two the best start we could. But with her back at the airline and this place only bringing in marginal profits . . ."

"Marginal? We're making more money than we ever have. Profits you don't have to lift a finger for."

"I've seen the numbers. Improvement, sure, but nobody's getting rich off this venture."

"I'm making a living, Dale. And my employees do too. But whatever, I'm not going to argue. If you want out, then I'll come up with the cash to buy you out. I've got some savings. Might make things tight for a while, but I'm sure Cass and I can talk about it and find a way to get you clear."

"I've spoken to Cassidy already. And I'm advising her to sell too."

A knot tightened in my stomach.

Dale laid his palms on the desk. "Truth is, with her back in Boston, she doesn't need this place anymore either. We talked it over and it sounds like you two aren't having any thoughts of getting back together. I think it's time she cuts ties and goes her own way."

"She's never expressed any interest in selling Archangel."

"Well, she told me she's considering it." He held up his hands. "And I know hers and my share would be too much capital to expect you to come up with out of your own pocket, that's why I went ahead and located another interested buyer."

"You what?"

"I've had a generous offer from another party who would love to work with you to build this brand into its full potential."

My mind was racing to avoid being buried in this avalanche of bullshit.

"NO," I said. "Archangel isn't for sale."

"This isn't a solo operation, Luke. You always agreed to partners."

"I agreed to be in business with *my wife,* and a *temporary* partnership with her father."

"But you couldn't follow through, could you, Luke? And sometimes plans have to change. I'd think you'd be happy to be out of a financial obligation to my family. A new partner could freshen up the place, new ideas, new directions."

"Who did you discuss this with?" I growled.

"Had a call from John Garbanza. He's a man with a lot of ideas."

"Johnny Overspray?" I choked out. "The guy's a two-bit used car salesman who wandered into aviation on a lark."

"He's doing a booming business in plane sales."

"He's a shark who slaps shitty paint jobs on high-time planes and bilks newbie pilots out of their money. Half the reason I do pre-purchase inspections is to help people steer clear of his unairworthy death traps."

"I've seen his numbers. He runs a highly profitable business."

"The guy won't even fly in the planes he sells."

"You don't need to be a pilot to be a good salesman."

"I only learned a few worthwhile things growing up with the dad I had, but one was: you don't buy a boat you haven't seen float. Same rule applies to planes. You don't get in one unless you know your mechanic would fill the back seat with their babies and do the same."

"Well, you can't fault the man just because he doesn't have children."

I rubbed a hand over my forehead. This conversation was going nowhere. Blackjack wandered in the door from whatever nocturnal adventures she'd been on and grazed my leg.

"This is a tense time for your family," I said, controlling my tone. "Let's come back to this once I've had a chance to talk to Cass. I'm sure there's a way we get you out of the business if you want out, but there's no way in hell I'm selling to Overspray."

Blackjack jumped onto the desk, but came to a quick halt at the sight of the man occupying my chair.

"We can discuss it further," he said, "but I think you'll need to adjust your expectations of what this place is going to be long-term. I know you and Cassidy had a vision for this business, but that's not the view anymore." He reached out to pet the cat and she hissed, causing him to jerk his hand back. He rose from the chair and straightened his shirt. "And maybe get some friendlier pets while you're at it."

He strode around the desk and out the door. When he was gone, it took all I had not to kick the door closed behind him.

EIGHT
WIDENING ARC

BLACKJACK PURRED as she rubbed a cheek across my knuckles. Her motor ran loud but it was well-tuned. The hum helped me focus. I had a plan for this morning and five minutes with Dale Dobbs wasn't going to derail me. There was a pile of log entries to sign in my physical inbox and no doubt a slew of emails to answer in my virtual one, but hanging around the office wasn't going to solve the most important problem of my day. I rubbed the cat's head one more time for luck, then got to work.

I had my gear loaded in short order and my Cessna 206 Stationaire amphibian was on the ramp ready to roll. Reese met me on the pilot's side as I was getting ready to climb up the pontoon.

"I'll be back in a few hours. Keep the guys busy."

"You going to tell me what's up?"

"Not yet. I'm sure it will get around. Everything does at this airport. But I don't need to be the one spreading it."

She nodded. Nosiness wasn't a character defect she dealt with. One of the many things I admired about her.

"Stay here, Murph," I said to the dog.

He looked forlorn, but I think he sensed this was no fishing trip.

By the time I was taxiing out to the runway, the sun was bright. I donned my sunglasses and took off into the glare on runway 7.

The growl of the 206's engine was smooth and powerful, a sound that hummed in your blood and never failed to please. Throttling forward on this seaplane was better on water but there were no bad takeoffs in this bird.

The tower granted my request for a right turn and I cruised south, overflying the tip of the peninsula and the dappled blue-green water around Fort De Soto. I stayed low, out of Tampa's airspace, and tracked toward the waypoint I'd programmed into my GPS. It was approximate, based on the last known location of Chris's Cessna 210.

Unlike my 206, Chris's plane didn't have floats and there was no good reason to be where he'd been, out past the Air Defense Identification Zone. When I hit the coast I called Flight Service and activated my flight plan. It hadn't been the easiest thing to file since I had no clear destination, but it would cover my ass when exiting and entering the ADIZ. Last thing I needed was a pair of F-22s streaking down from Tydall to investigate me. As a general rule, NORAD mostly cared about flights penetrating the country's air defense zone from elsewhere, and not domestic flights wiggling their way out, but discretion being the better part of valor, I knew when to keep the good guys pointing their missiles at the right targets. A little transparency can go a long way.

The water of the gulf was a turquoise that darkened into deep blue the farther west I flew. Seas were calm and the clouds were scattered. I intercepted the track Chris had flown and followed it as closely as I could.

Imagining what might have been going through his head was

difficult. It would have been a different scene, flying into the darkness, the horizon hard to distinguish. Night flight over water can muddle the senses, disorient a pilot to the point of vertigo.

It had been cloudier two nights ago. The stars being obscured would have made the gulf even more of a void. Distances felt vague in conditions like that. The glow of instruments from the 210's instrument panel would have been the only light. What was Chris using to navigate? The line on Flight Aware had been relatively straight, no wandering. If you are depressed and flying off into oblivion, do you still worry about holding a heading? Chris was a decent pilot but I didn't think of him as rigid. I had to think that if I was flying off into the night to end it all, I might get loose with my headings. But I was no expert on depression. Maybe he'd picked a heading and set the autopilot to hold it for him.

What else could you get to this direction? Key West maybe. That was about the only thing even vaguely this way. Until you hit Mexico.

I checked my fuel gauges. The 210 and the 206 were similar airplanes with comparable fuel capacity. Chris would have cruised faster with his landing gear stowed and no bulky floats dragging in the wind, so he'd have plenty of range, but it all depended on how much he'd left with.

I scanned the water, dipping low and making slow turns. A lot of variables were in play out here. There was no way to know how hard the 210 would have hit the water if it went down, no way to tell what would have floated. Prevailing currents would have sent anything floating east, but even if he'd ditched the plane in level seas and got out, this was a long way from shore. The parts of me that harbored hope were staying quiet.

A blip on my traffic avoidance system piqued my interest and I spotted the Coast Guard Jayhawk a few moments later. It was low over the water but moving. The sight took me back. The

MH-60T was a variant on the UH60 Blackhawks I'd flown in the Army. The orange-and-white paint scheme might be different, but the helicopter performed the way it was designed to no matter the branch. As I watched, the Jayhawk dipped forward, tilting the main rotor and moving off toward shore. I turned the yoke and wagged my wings as it passed, but got no response from the other aircraft.

A knot in my gut made me think that was the aircraft I ought to still be in. Old habits die hard. I caught myself rubbing at the scar under my jaw and put my hand back on the throttle.

An aircraft was just a tool. I had one at my fingertips too and I intended to use it. I pressed the yoke forward and dove toward the water.

The 206 was an easy plane to handle and I had no qualms about skimming the surface with it. I did passes of varying altitudes in widening circles from the last known location of the 210, but only spotted a few dolphins and fishing charters for my efforts. The boats flared some hope in me. This wasn't so far out that it was untraveled, but it was a lot of water to be lost in. I knew Chris didn't have a raft because the one he usually borrowed when he needed it was currently in the seat behind me. There was a survival kit next to it too, plus water bottles and a few things I'd use in the unlikely event of locating a survivor out here.

I tried to get into his head, imagine the friend I knew cashing it all in. What could have driven him to it? The longer I tried to answer, the more objections I came up with. No part of me could rectify the discrepancies between the man I knew and the one who might have done this. But I suppose we never really know what it's like inside another person's head.

As the morning wore on and my fuel tanks lightened, my chances of doing any good dwindled. I marked my progress on the tablet I'd brought along, then finally pushed the throttle back to full power and climbed away from the water. Reaching the coast again felt like failure. I'd done what I could but it didn't feel like much.

Nobody expected me to be out here.

My conscience ought to be clear, but the nagging in my gut had only grown during the flight. Through every innumerable circle I'd made over the water, my doubts about Chris's unexpected disappearance had only multiplied, and my failure to find the plane or my old friend hadn't given me answers. It just gave me more questions.

NINE
CROWDED

THE LUNCHTIME CROWD hanging around Hangar 4 was larger than usual today. We always had a few extra bodies in the place by noon, but today the break corner was downright packed. The regulars were primarily old dudes who enjoyed cold cuts and reminiscing. Most days I'd spend a few minutes chatting with the group, but today I knew they'd be asking me to relive the Seneca landing and I wasn't in the mood. After putting away the 206, I made my excuses and climbed the stairs to my office alone.

A stack of to-do items loomed on my desk so I fired up my computer. Archangel Aviation wasn't going to run itself. The office phone had gathered a half dozen voicemails in my absence and my email had accrued five times that many. I had a part-time office assistant, but she'd been home three days with a feverish kid. I'd rather have my eyelashes yanked out than open email most days, but someone had to do it.

I skimmed over the inbox headers to assess the most pressing issues, wandering down the rabbit hole of items I'd missed from the previous few days. I froze when I spotted a message from Chris Carter in the mix from Wednesday. I'd skimmed over the email yesterday, assuming it could wait, but that was before I knew he was missing. I opened it now and read.

The message was normal enough for Chris. Letting me know he'd be stopping by for the logs. He asked if the new transmitter for his left fuel tank had come in. Wondered if there was a chance it would be in that day. He'd asked the same thing when I saw him in-person Wednesday night now that I thought about it. Not an odd query. The plane's fuel gauge read inaccurately and we'd finally isolated the issue. He'd been itching to have it resolved. But why care if you were planning to fly the plane off into the gulf and spiral it into the water?

You wouldn't.

Could the crash have been an accident? But then why leave a suicide note on the phone?

Too many things weren't adding up for me.

I closed the email and tried to focus on business. I didn't get more than a few emails in before the phone rang.

"Archangel Aviation."

The woman's voice on the phone was even and clear. "Mr. Angel, this is Detective Blake Rivers with the Saint Petersburg police. I'm following up on a report of a missing person, do you have a minute to talk?"

"Ah. Sure." I leaned back in my chair.

"I'd like to meet at some point to go over some details, but if you would be able to verify a few points from the report for me now, I'd appreciate it."

"No problem."

"The report states you did work on Dr. Carter's plane recently. Can you tell me what that was?"

"Troubleshooting a fuel indicator issue. Ordered a part for the repair."

"Was the aircraft safe to fly with that issue?"

"Chris was aware of it. Wasn't a safety concern if you kept

track of your fuel consumption manually. And the other fuel tank gauge read okay."

"Any other maintenance issues with the aircraft that you were dealing with?"

"None that Chris had brought to my attention. The plane's next annual inspection wasn't due till September."

"Has anyone else worked on Dr. Carter's plane recently?"

"Not that I know of."

"Were you aware of an intention by Dr. Carter to sell the aircraft?"

"No."

"Okay. One more thing. During your conversation Wednesday night, he didn't give any indication of where he was flying or who he might be meeting?"

"I didn't even know he was going up." The phone was quiet for a long beat. "So, no news on his whereabouts?"

"We're doing all we can to locate Dr. Carter," she replied. "About meeting with you in person, Mr. Angel—when would be a good time?"

"I'm around here till at least five-thirty most nights."

"I'll stop by tonight," she replied. "I appreciate your cooperation."

When I replaced the handset, I couldn't help feeling I'd somehow landed myself under a microscope.

It was fine. The maintenance on the plane was solid. I knew that much.

I attempted to refocus my attention on work but it was no good. I gave up and walked back downstairs.

One whistle for Murphy and he came bounding to me.

Reese was pulling back into the parking lot on her motorcycle as I went to my Jeep.

"More places to be today?" She cut the ignition and swung the kick stand down.

"I'll be back. I'm headed over to Venetian Isles. Need to visit somebody."

"Something to do with your ex-father-in-law being here this morning?"

"Actually going to talk to Ava."

Reese furrowed her brow. "Harper's mom? I thought you two hated each other."

"I *don't* hate her. I just avoid her."

"Have fun then." She slung her helmet over her handlebars and strode off toward the shop.

Murphy scrambled into the back seat of my Jeep with a little help. The Wrangler fired up and settled to a low rumble. The lack of doors or roof on the vehicle made for a noisy ride, but it made up for it by also being blistering hot.

Cruising the waterfront helped the temperature some, and before long I'd worked my way into the Venetian Isles neighborhood, a historic and pricey spot not far off the bay.

The neighborhood was home to old trees and a fair amount of old money, though there were people like the Carters back here too. Chris did all right as a plastic surgeon, but he'd come from modest means. Still, their place sat on a cul-de-sac that backed up against a channel. Getting out to open water required passing under several low bridges, so it ruled out sailboat ownership, but Chris had kept a flats boat at his dock.

Pulling up to the place brought back memories of early morning fishing runs. It had been years since the last one. The dock stood empty now.

Cassidy's rental car was in the driveway so I parked on the street.

Murphy immediately set to investigating the front shrubbery, checking the notifications from local dogs and leaving a few of his own. I cut across the lawn and climbed three steps to the front door.

The chime from the doorbell was musical. Some peppy pop tune I vaguely recognized from TV commercials.

When the door opened, it was my stunner ex-wife on the other side of the door. She'd changed out of her airline uniform and was wearing a tank top and jean shorts that left a distracting amount of her tanned thighs visible.

"Luke. What are you doing here?"

"Need to talk to Ava."

She put a hand to her hip. "I don't know if that's a good idea. I doubt she wants to see you right now."

I spotted the back of a child's head over a distant couch.

"Hey, Harp."

The head turned. "Uncle Luke?"

A rustling from the bushes was the only warning before Murphy shot up the steps at full speed and was past Cassidy's legs in a flash.

"Oh geez," Cassidy muttered, barely dodging the furry cannonball.

A squeak of delight came from inside as the dog located Harper.

"Murphy!" My niece's voice hit an octave reserved solely for greeting dogs or finding out she was going to a theme park. I could make out the sound of Murphy's tail thumping the furniture all the way from the porch.

Cassidy sighed and opened the door a little farther. "Fine. That's a cheap trick, but it's effective. May as well come in."

I made an effort to keep the smirk off my face, but I made a note to give Murphy one of the good treats once no one was looking.

Dogs and kids. Worked every time.

TEN

AVA

HARPER CARTER WAS one of my favorite humans. Some kids have a natural joy for life that's contagious and she was one. Her light was dimmed today, but I could still catch it in the way she was playing with Murphy.

Life had dealt her family a tough blow, but she wasn't down for the count yet. Hope still shone in her bright eyes. She was tall for eleven, hitting that gangly knees phase of childhood, but it didn't take much to see the beauty she'd soon grow into as a teenager. She wore bright colors, and last I'd checked, she hadn't succumbed to the angst of her preteen peers yet.

She hugged me with both arms when I made it inside.

"I think you've grown an inch this year," I said.

"I'm the tallest on my volleyball team."

"Good sport for you. When's the season start again?"

"Not till September." She made it sound like it was an eternity. "I'm doing it for summer camp though too."

"Good. And I see you're still adding to your collection." I gestured to the dozen multicolored friendship bracelets around each wrist.

"Coach makes me take them off for games, which is lame. You want me to make you one? I've got some designs for guys too. I made one for my dad." Her face grew serious. "You heard about Dad?"

"Yeah. Going to see what we can figure out."

"Was something wrong with his plane?"

"Not that I know of, kiddo."

"Coast Guard is looking for him, right?"

"Sure are. Saw the helicopters this morning."

"You think maybe they found him, but they just haven't told us yet?"

I rested a hand on her shoulder. "I'm confident everybody is searching hard."

"I could go with you in your plane. To help look. Dad's been giving me lessons. I can start it and do the taxi and the takeoff. I can't do landing yet, but I'm really good at the starting. I like the part where I get to yell out the window and say 'Clear prop!' I do it really loud."

The voice from the doorway was low but firm. "Nobody is getting in a plane right now."

I turned to find Ava Carter in the doorway to the hall. She was wearing leggings and a St. Pete Krav Maga studio T-shirt. Her light brown hair was down. I wasn't used to seeing her without makeup. She looked tired and held an empty coffee mug. Cassidy moved around the kitchen island and went to her, taking the coffee mug and heading to the coffee pot with it.

Ava followed the activity vaguely, then her eyes fell on me again.

"What do you want, Luke?"

"Checking in."

"The police said you took them to the hangar."

Cassidy set the refilled coffee mug on the counter in reach of

Ava and turned to Harper. "Harp, why don't we go outside, get some fresh air."

"I want to hear," Harper replied.

"Go outside," her mother commanded.

Harper crossed her arms. "But what if it's important? I should know too."

I pulled a couple of dog biscuits from my pocket and held them out to her. "Hey. If you take care of Murph for a few minutes outside, I promise I'll come out after and we can talk about whatever you want."

Harper looked skeptical, but grudgingly held out a hand for the biscuits. Murphy spun in place and did a little hop. Harper's first move toward the sliding door had Murphy racing for it, and she'd barely cracked it open before he nosed through and bolted for the back yard. Cassidy gave her sister a wan smile and followed.

Ava studied me in silence.

"Want to sit?" I offered.

She took a look at the coffee on the counter that her sister had poured her, but left it there when she moved into the sitting area of the living room. She took the couch so I parked myself in a nearby armchair.

"He tell you anything when you saw him?" Ava said. She was watching me carefully.

"Said he was stopping by for the maintenance records. Something for the insurance. Didn't think anything of it. Now I know I missed something."

Ava nodded. "He probably didn't want to tell you. He was supposed to sell it."

I narrowed my eyes. "Sell the 210? Since when?"

"Because it was a waste of money. The hangar, the upkeep. It was all too much expense. Same with that damned boat, though I think we used that more often."

"You guys having financial trouble?"

Her arms were crossed. One leg over the other. A closed book. "He didn't use that plane enough to justify it. That's what we decided. It was what was best for our future."

"Sorry to hear that. But why not tell me? I could have helped."

"Because you'd have talked him out of it."

"Not if it was the right decision. Sounds like you'd worked it out."

She finally relaxed her shoulders and sighed. "You know how much he loved that plane. I thought it was best if he went through someone else, because you would have offered him other solutions and it wouldn't have solved the real problem."

"He needed cash."

She sighed and looked toward the kitchen. "You probably heard about the lawsuit last year. The stupid butt implant chick who claimed she fell off a ladder because her ass was lopsided?"

"Heard something about it."

"That woman had the IQ of a walnut, but her lawyers were sharks. The settlement hit Chris's practice hard. His loans from medical school were always enormous. We still haven't paid off *my* loans from my degree. Harper's school isn't cheap . . . . I thought we'd be better off by now. Then he took a risk on a *stupid* investment."

"Stocks?"

"No. *Crypto.*"

She said it like the word tasted foul in her mouth.

"He had this friend who swore on these things, some ridiculous new ones. Entrava? Eternius? I can't even pronounce them. Some currencies his buddy promised were going big. He had this system of buying and selling he said he was making a killing with. Showed Chris a bunch of spreadsheets. Turns out the both of them lost their shirts. You know Chris was never the best judge of people."

That part I did know.

"Never marry for looks, right?" She gave another exasperated sigh.

"How much did he invest?"

"Too much. More than he told me he was going to. I was furious."

She stared at the ceiling for a moment. When she lowered her gaze there were tears in her eyes. "But it wasn't so bad that he should have done what he did. We could have fixed it, we could have—" Her voice cracked and her lip quivered.

Shit.

I slid off the armchair and moved to the seat next to her. Not touching her, but closer. I snagged a tissue from a box on the end table. Offered it.

Ava took the tissue and dabbed at her nose. She turned toward me. "I didn't think he was taking it *that* hard. I was mad, but we had a plan."

"It's not your fault."

"It might be."

I rested a hand on her shoulder. "It isn't. I promise you."

She shuddered and turned toward me. "I'm so tired of not knowing. He left that note. He said he was done. Like nothing even mattered anymore. Our life, our daughter." She whimpered and pressed her head to my shoulder. I rubbed a couple of circles on her back, then took a grip on the back of the couch. She finally sat up straighter.

The air conditioning came on, blowing at us from an overhead vent. Ava balled up the last of her tissue.

"Do you think he died quickly?" The question was so quiet I almost missed it.

"Yeah . . . maybe . . . I don't know what happened. To be

honest, this has me all turned around. Doesn't make any sense." I leaned forward, resting my elbows on my knees, and stared at the carpet. "When Chris came down to the airport Wednesday night, he told you he was coming to see me to get the logs?"

Ava nodded. "He actually practiced what he was going to say."

"He was that worried about me talking him out of it?"

"You know how much he idolized you. I think half the reason he had that plane was because you had one."

"I doubt that."

"I'm serious. He hated the idea of not living up to you. It was like you were his big brother or something."

The words churned in my stomach.

"Big brothers aren't all they're cracked up to be. And Chris was a badass all on his own. He was a damned doctor."

"Yeah, well. He looked up to you. 'Cool Hand Luke.' I've never even seen that movie, but that's what he'd call you. I think he might have been the most disappointed when you and Cass split."

I glanced toward the sliding door to the back yard. I could just glimpse Cassidy in a patio chair. The sun lit her face and she looked damned near luminous. "He had some competition there."

Ava looked out the door too. Harper came into view with the dog.

"I don't want Harper harboring too much hope. I didn't tell her about the note yet and she still thinks there's a chance Chris is coming back. But don't lie to her, okay?"

In the quiet, I could make out a few happy barks from Murphy.

"I won't."

Ava rubbed her palms over her knees. "A police detective is coming back soon. I should probably get myself together."

I stood.

Ava got off the couch. She rested a hand on my forearm momentarily, then walked into the kitchen. She poured herself a glass of water before heading for the hallway door. I moved to the other side of the kitchen and watched Harper toss a stick to Murphy.

"Luke?"

I turned.

Ava was in the doorway to the hall.

"Yeah."

"Things got complicated during the divorce. And when Chris and I were having trouble . . . I know I said some things to you that weren't . . . ."

"Don't worry about it."

"I appreciate that you never said anything to anyone."

"You were going through a rough time. We all were. But no harm done."

"I've never thought you were a bad guy. Maybe not right for Cassidy. But I'm not one to say anything, am I?" She fidgeted with the edge of her water cup. "Anyway. I don't want you to think I despise you. Because I don't."

"Don't worry about it. I don't hate you either. Life's too short." The words were out of my mouth before I could catch myself.

But she nodded. "Yeah. It is, isn't it."

She brushed a hand under her eye and caught the beginnings of a tear, then turned and walked away.

I kicked myself.

Cassidy and Harper were both watching me through the sliding glass door. I forced a smile back on my face and walked out to join them.

ELEVEN
HARPER

MY EX-WIFE and my niece had a lot in common, though not all of it was apparent at first glance. They shared a family resemblance of fair features and natural athleticism, but it had been a strength of spirit that first attracted me to Cassidy, especially as she had forged a path in a career still heavily skewed toward men. Her persistence in climbing the ladder as a pilot in the airlines was something I admired, even though the lifestyle was a notable factor in the demise of our marriage.

Harper's inner strength showed in her commitment to sports. Despite never being the standout in skill, she was the most likely to work hard with a positive attitude, something her smarter coaches valued more than innate talent. Her positivity had a galvanizing effect on her teammates and she rushed into action with so much enthusiasm that no one ever wanted to disappoint her. One coach said she had the ability to "lead from the middle." And I found that as apt a description of her influence as any.

Out in the yard playing with Murphy, it was easy to peg her as a normal kid. But this situation was anything but normal. The fact that she was holding it together so well wasn't lost on me. It was yet another indication that she had the guts to face tough circumstances, and it's why when she spoke to me, I gave her my full attention.

"Are you going to go look for Dad?"

"Went out this morning for a bit."

"I know mom says she doesn't want anybody in a plane, but I'd go anyway. Dad would do it for us."

"He most certainly would. And whatever there is to be done, we'll do it."

Cassidy chimed in. "And we are here for you, whatever *you* need. We'll get through it together."

"What if it was bad guys?" Harper's hands formed a knot as she wrung them in front of her. "I was thinking, what if it was someone bad that like, took Dad and they want to hold him for ransom or something? You were in the Army, right? Does that mean you can go after them?"

"We don't know enough yet to think anyone else was involved."

Harper studied me. "But if it is bad guys, you could stop them, right? Does being in the Army mean you have a gun?"

I shared a glance with Cassidy, "Look, Harp. I'm not the police, but the police will do all they can to look into it. If we get any indication someone is involved, they'll be all over it."

"My social studies teacher says police departments are historically under-budget."

I sighed. "Sometimes. It doesn't mean they don't do the job. They are going to do everything they can to figure out what happened. You can talk to your aunt about it, her boyfriend is in law enforcement. He'd know more than me."

Cassidy inhaled sharply and something tightened in her posture.

"Aunt Cass's boyfriend broke up with her. That's why he's not here."

That was news. Cassidy was making a point of not looking at me.

"Gotcha," I muttered. "Hadn't heard that. But whatever the case, the police will be helping every way they can,"

"I heard what those cops said. They think he did it on his own."

"It's still too early to know anything for sure. They're going to investigate."

"Do *you* think Dad left us?"

The question was blunt, but there was a lot of vulnerability behind it. Her eyes didn't stray from mine.

"Your dad loved you, kiddo. As true as the sun rises. Don't ever doubt it. Whatever happened doesn't change that."

Her bright eyes were glistening more than usual but no tears escaped. The kid was holding it together like a champ.

"Will you promise me that if it's bad guys, that you'll get them? Will you save Dad?"

"We're all going to do everything we can."

"But you *know* us better than the police do. Even though you and Aunt Cass got divorced, you'll still help us, right? I trust you more than them."

I shifted my feet and glanced at Cassidy, but she was keeping her mouth shut. I faced Harper, stooping to be closer to her level. "If there's something I can do, I'll do it."

She put her hand out.

The gesture was simple. A pact. A promise.

I took her hand and she pumped it once. "Okay."

She glanced to Cassidy, then back to me, a look of accomplishment on her face. Her intent was clear. We were in this together now.

"I'm going to go tell mom." She didn't wait for approval, just sprinted for the house, vanishing through the sliding door so quickly that even Murphy didn't have time to follow.

I turned to Cassidy. "I feel like I've been drafted."

"She's eleven. She needs to feel like she's doing something."

"Kid's got a lot of heart."

"Usually I'd say that's a good thing. But this is going to be extra hard for her." Cassidy put her hands in her pockets. I noticed she'd gained a friendship bracelet since this morning too.

My phone buzzed and I pulled it from my pocket.

The notification name said Marie.

>>> Still thinking about last night. It was that good.

I shoved the phone back into my pocket.

Cassidy was studying me. "Another hot date?"

I thought I'd kept my face impassive reading the text but she could always read me like a book.

"Something I'll deal with later."

A breeze rustled the palms and brought the scent of jasmine from the neighbor's yard. It blew some of Cassidy's hair into her face. I resisted the urge to help her with it. She brushed it behind her ear herself.

We stood in silence for a few moments. The quiet somehow made the loss deeper. Chris, but also the gulf that now stood between Cassidy and me. Without Harper, the space was wider, more obvious.

"Sorry about the Vince comment earlier. I didn't know."

"Don't worry about it. He's been gone for a while." She crossed her arms under her breasts. "Did my dad talk to you?"

"Yeah. That was an unpleasant ambush to walk into this morning."

Cass's mouth tightened. "I came to give you a heads up at the boat, but your extra curricular activities made things difficult."

"I'm not selling any part of Archangel. That wasn't our deal. We said we'd keep it together till I could raise the cash to buy your dad out."

"We didn't ever plan for *this* eventuality." She gestured toward the house.

"What does it change? Chris doing whatever he did doesn't affect our business arrangement."

"You don't think so? You don't think coming to the airport is going to feel different? For Harper? For Ava? It used to be the place of fun family memories, and now it's going to be the place Harper's dad flew off and killed himself."

"We don't know that for sure."

"*We're* not eleven, Luke. I'm not going to sugarcoat this."

"Archangel was more than just a business for us. It's not something we jettison at the first sign of difficulty."

"First sign? You don't think divorcing me counted as a speed bump in our business plan?

"*You* divorced *me*. It was your idea."

"And you could have put up some kind of fight, couldn't you? But no. You were happy to go right back to being single like us being married never happened."

"I gave you what you wanted."

"No. You pretended everything was fine, like you always do. Made me be the bad guy."

Murphy whined. He was laying with his head on his paws, eyes on both of us.

I sighed. "I didn't come here to fight."

"Of course not. That would involve emotional effort."

I glared at her. Then turned away. Her words stung, but truth does that.

"Come on, Murph. Time to go."

Murphy got up and walked with me but his tail was low. We skipped the house and went straight for the side gate to the front yard. Cassidy was still standing there with her arms crossed when I turned to look back.

"We'll talk about this later," I said. "When it's better timing. I'm going back to work."

I closed the gate behind me and cut across the lawn to my Jeep. I'd just climbed in when I heard tapping on glass. I looked up to find Harper at the second-story window overlooking the driveway. She waved, then gave me a thumbs up.

Leading from the middle.

I took a deep breath and gave her a thumbs up in reply. Then I started the Jeep and took off. As the house receded in the rear view mirror, I had the vague feeling of bugging out of the battlefield after taking fire. But this wasn't relief. It felt like I was leaving the wounded behind.

TWELVE

TURF BATTLE

YOU GET to know the regulars at an airport once you've been there a while. There are the avid young flight students, intermediate level instructors, veteran instructors, mechanics, apprentice mechanics, and a whole bunch of retired dudes who just like to hang around and escape the boredom of home. A bunch of other people work the airport in capacities from counter personnel to city maintenance.

The vehicles they arrive in range from bicycles to electric scooters, battered pickup trucks to this year's model SUVs. On weekends you might see some antiques out. The cars mostly, but sometimes the drivers too. The people who like old planes are often the same people who like old cars. It's not unusual to open a hangar door and find a classic T-bird or a vintage Triumph tucked under the wing of a plane from the same era.

Getting to know all these vehicles gives you the ability to recognize the newcomers. That's why when I entered airport property and drove past the outside parking lot for Hangar 3, the Lamborghini Aventador stuck out like a dick on a forehead. Hard not to when it was painted matte gold. If you were blind enough to miss the over-the-top styling of the car, the vanity license plate usually settled it. The text read BIG DLZ.

I pulled up to my hangar and parked the Jeep. Murphy immediately sprinted for his water bowl but I didn't head inside yet. I walked to the fence and stared into the blackened soul of the Lamborghini's interior. The windows were tinted but not enough that I hadn't been able to spot Johnny Overspray with his phone up taking pictures of something in the direction of my hangar.

"Hey! Come out here." I shouted through the chain link that divided where I was from the exterior parking lot. The figure inside was frozen. I pointed at him.

Finally the scissor door opened—a ridiculous display on its own—like a peacock fanning its tail. When John Garbanza climbed out, he looked the part too, with a floral patterned suit and mirrored shades. He had his AirPods in and didn't bother to pull them out to address me.

"Luke Angel! Just the guy I was hoping to see. How have you been, my man?" He gave me the ten-thousand-watt grin he no doubt practiced in the mirror at home.

"What are you doing here, Johnny?"

"Just checking things out. Been ages since I've come by your shop."

He certainly hadn't been invited.

"Heard you've been talking to Dale Dobbs. I don't appreciate you conducting business behind my back."

He spread his hands. "What was behind your back? We've just been talking. Dale's a great guy, looking to make some changes. I'm excited about what he has in mind. He has vision."

Johnny walked to the pedestrian gate and fumbled with the code box. "I always forget the combo for this damned thing." I let him fight with it while I considered how long it would take for him to find it in his phone. As much as he deserved to stand in the sun and sweat in that ridiculous suit, I didn't have that kind of time. I yanked the gate open.

"Thanks, bro."

Johnny was nearly my height and conventionally handsome, but up close he looked over-tanned, and you could grease a wheel bearing with the amount of product he wore in his hair. His brow was damp. Maybe the Aventador needed its AC serviced.

He gestured toward the hangar. "Saw you painted the Stationaire. That's a great plane. Decent avionics? I bet I could get you six-hundred K for that."

"My plane's not for sale."

"Sure. Right. Just saying, this market, I bet you could make a killing, even on an older model like that. Saw you have something else in the back, what is that, a Commander?" He walked around me to see.

"You want to ogle airplanes, look all you want, but nothing is for sale. Neither is the business."

"Don't get defensive, Luke. I know how much sweat equity you've got in this place. But maybe you think about how much a partnership with someone like me could benefit you. You've got a decent reputation for your work. With a little marketing savvy, you could really start crushing the competition."

He put his hands on his hips and squared up with my hangar. "It's a killer space. If you put a sign up street side, maybe with some lights? I could get a camera crew down here, run some ads. Optically you're in great shape with the people you've got working here." He dropped his voice lower. "You know, the gay chick and the young black guy. All the libs eat that shit up. Maybe we put some bios on the website. People love an underdog story, especially if he's from the wrong side of the tracks or whatnot."

"That's Tyson Martin," I growled. "His grandfather used to *own* Bayside Aviation. He's not from the wrong side of anything."

"Like Hank Martin? The old dude everybody talks about? I heard that guy was loaded."

"If you think doctoring up a website is what gets people in the door here, you know less about aviation than I thought you did. We get more business than we can accept already because Reese is the best troubleshooter I've ever met, and this crew gets shit done right. If you found a more experienced pilot than Rip or a more motivated worker than Tyson, I'd eat that ridiculous jacket you have on. But you won't, and that's why you and I aren't going into business together."

Johnny put up his hands. "Dude, I get you. No one is saying change any of that. But what about expand on it? I've got a few guys that are ace too. Been working with them for years. Quick, cheap, they know how to whip through a project. Together, we could really pump some cash through this place."

I sighed.

There was an old saying in the maintenance business. You could have it cheap, fast, or good, but you only got to pick two. Whichever two you picked, it couldn't be the other. I knew exactly which factor that left out in Johnny's system.

"I'm going to let you in on a secret," Johnny said, leaning in. He had his phone out and swiped to a photo. "I've got an investor, dynamite guy, heard what you've been doing here and wants to drop some major dough. Wants a guy with *your* skills at the wheel. And we're talking big money. And it's cash." He flipped the phone around and held it up.

The photo showed stacks of cash piled on someone's table. Looked like a bank got robbed.

"You ever seen that much cheddar? That's five mil, my man."

"Who leaves five million dollars lying around on a table?"

Johnny laughed. "I had to buy a special safe for it."

"You're holding that?"

"Bananas, right? My investor hates banks. I said, whatever you want."

Bananas wasn't the word I had in mind. Idiotic maybe. Dangerous. Bad decision making somewhere, especially if they were trusting this goon with it.

"Listen to me, Johnny. If and when the time comes, and Dale really wants out, *I'll* buy him out. But I don't need you flashing pictures of cash at him and putting ideas in his head. He's dealing with a lot right now."

"You're talking about the Chris Carter thing?"

I narrowed my eyes. "How'd you know about it?"

"The plane going off into the gulf? Tragic isn't it? So sad. Heartbreaking really. Guess he was really messed up in the head." Johnny looked up to the sky, as if Chris was floating around up there.

"He seemed fine the night I saw him. Just in a hurry."

"Probably off his meds. I hear a lot of doctors self-prescribe these days. Read a Twitter article about it. It's an epidemic."

"Ava said Chris was feeling pressure to sell his plane. That pressure coming from you?"

"Pressure? Is that what you think I do? People come to me, not the other way around. Chris was talking to me about selling. Well, actually, it was Ava who called me. She knew I could get him top dollar. But we never closed the deal. Too bad for him, I guess."

The fact that it had been Ava pushing Chris to Johnny didn't surprise me. But Johnny even talking about Chris was leaving a sour taste in my mouth. "So Dale told you about the disappearance, or Ava, or who?"

"What? Oh, yeah, Dale. Really close family too from what I can tell. Ava and Chris had a little kid, you know that? Hannah." He put his hands to his hips again. "Too bad about the kid. It's always a shit-show when girls lose a dad at that age. Probably end up a stripper now or something."

My fists clenched at the same time as my jaw.

"But she'll do all right if she grows those big titties like her mama."

My hands were on his jacket so fast I didn't even recall reacting. I just shoved Johnny toward the exit. "Get the hell out of here."

"Hey! Whoa! What the hell?"

I gave him a harder shove and he bounced off the chain link. One of his AirPods fell out.

"You crazy?" Johnny righted himself and got his balance back. He was a fit guy, and for a second he looked like he was going to put his fists up, but he must have thought better of it. A pity. I would've welcomed the excuse.

He glanced behind me.

Reese had wandered a few feet out of the hangar with a long Snap-On wrench hanging loosely from one hand.

"I'm going already," Johnny muttered. "Shit. We were just having a *conversation.*" He stooped and scooped up his earbud.

There were a lot of things I wanted to shout at him but I kept my jaw clamped shut.

"You need to get a grip on that temper of yours, Luke-y boy. De-stress or something." He finished putting the earpiece back in and straightened his cuffs. "You're lucky I'm not the litigious type. This is a six-thousand dollar suit."

"Then maybe you shouldn't wear it to an airplane hangar."

"Excuse me for thinking I was dealing with a professional. I guess that's beyond you."

I forcibly unclenched my fists once he was through the gate. He shot me another accusing glare as he climbed into the Lamborghini. When it started, he kept it at a ridiculous RPM even in reverse. When he shifted into first he lurched but tried to make up for it while turning into the street. He blasted out of the driveway and tore down the street at a high pitched whine, missing the cues to shift till the engine was redlining.

Reese was at my elbow by the time the car disappeared. "Guy's going to burn up that motor."

"I'm sure he'll wrap it around a pole before that, the way he drives."

"Don't sound so enthusiastic about it. People will be onto you."

She met my eye and I couldn't help but smirk. "Thanks for having my back. You angling for a raise or something?"

"Who me?" She scratched her temple with the wrench. "I was just taking a fresh-air break. You could trash that guy in your sleep. That's the salesman you hate?"

"I don't hate anybody. I just have a strong dislike for a few people."

"Deep-seated loathing."

"Mild irritation."

"Keep telling yourself that. Just know that when all your repressed rage eventually comes out, I'll be excited to see it." She swatted me on the shoulder.

We turned around and faced Hangar 4. Something about the sight of it grounded me. I let out a breath. "Chris Carter is missing. Probably dead."

"Knew it had to be something bad."

"There's something wrong about it, though. Doesn't make sense."

"You getting dragged into the drama?"

"Didn't want to be. But I promised Harper I'd look into it. She deserves answers."

"What do you need?"

"Just some time. I know it will put more on your shoulders here."

She shrugged.

"Keep an eye out for that guy, will you? I want to know if he comes back."

"I'll zip tie him to a propeller for you so you can punch him again when you get back."

"I didn't punch him."

"Five bucks says you do eventually."

I grunted.

Wasn't the worst thing I could think of doing with my time. But for that to happen, things would have to start going my way.

THIRTEEN
ATTACKED

I'D MANAGED to get in a few hours of actual work by the time five-fifteen rolled around. Tyson was the first to let me know it was past quitting time, knocking on my office door and stirring me from the pile of customer invoices and log entries.

"I'm headed out, boss."

"Sounds good, Ty. Nice work today."

He and Reese had successfully jacked Keith's Seneca II and released the landing gear. A quick inspection had shown the issue with the jammed gear door mechanism and I had the parts ordered. They'd get into the repairs soon, and so far, it was looking good. Barry and Keith had bonded over the whole "crash landing" experience and were best buddies now. They'd spent the afternoon in the flight school lobby regaling student pilots with the tale. But it was Reese and Tyson doing most of the hard work.

I leaned back in my chair. "Hey, let's carve out some time tomorrow to get you the rest of that tailwheel time in. You still want that sign-off, right?"

Tyson perked up. "Yeah? That'd be fire."

"We'll take the 185, figure out some grass strips to bounce it around on."

"I'm all for that. You all good here? You need me to stay late tonight?"

"Nah, get out of here. I'm set."

Tyson was smiling on his way out. Good kid. He was a newly minted airframe mechanic and had earned his private pilot's license. He'd have better-paying offers soon, but I was hoping I could keep him around a while longer.

I got out of my chair and stretched. Murphy scrambled out of his dog bed and did the same, ready to do something more fun.

"Okay. If you insist." I took a frisbee off the top of the file cabinet and he leapt with all four paws in his excitement. I barely had the office door open before he was out and scrambling down the stairs. The landing at the top of the stairs had a railing I could lean on and overlook the hangar. Murphy made it to the main door and spun in place. I chucked the frisbee and it soared all the way out of the hangar and curved toward the ramp. Murphy disappeared after it in a blur.

I meandered down the stairs to follow, expecting the dog to come racing back any second, but Murphy didn't immediately reappear. It took me the better part of a minute to get outside. Murphy had dropped the frisbee partway back from wherever he'd caught it and was staring out at the parking lot. He let out a low growl.

It wasn't uncommon for walkers and bikers to come down this road, often with dogs, so distractions for Murphy were common. But this time there were no dogs in sight. There was a car though. A faded-green early 2000s Honda sedan with an aftermarket exhaust that made it sound like an idling jet. The high pitched whine was likely even more annoying for Murphy's ears. The car had dark window tint all the way around and it was difficult to make out the occupants. No one I knew, but a snout slammed into the back passenger window with an eruption of barking and snarls that made me jolt. Bared teeth raged against the glass in a smear of saliva.

Murphy barked back, but the slobbering beast in the back of that car wanted us dead.

"Come on, Murph. Let's close up."

Murphy quit his barking and retrieved his frisbee, then trotted over while I activated the switch for the hangar door. As I stared out at the parking lot, the old Honda pulled out of its parking space and back onto the road, but instead of heading west toward the public access, it turned east.

There was nothing that way except the Coast Guard base and one more airport gate near the Civil Air Patrol. Occasionally a mechanic applicant from the local tech school would get lost looking for the test examiners that way. I checked my watch. It was a little late to be starting an exam.

The sun was still up and I'd refueled the 206, so I figured I might do another hour or two out over the water, but as of yet, I'd seen no sign of Detective Rivers for our scheduled chat. If she didn't show up soon, I'd abandon hope.

There had been no good news from the Coast Guard yet, and odds were long on any optimistic scenario. But I'd told Harper I'd do what I could, so I'd keep looking.

Murphy was still lingering near the bushes outside when I got the hangar door closed. I putzed around the hangar another few minutes tidying things and setting up the coffee maker for the next day before heading out to the plane. I looked around for Murphy when I got outside but the dog wasn't in evidence.

"Hey, Murph!"

I waited for the familiar scratching of claws on asphalt.

Nothing.

"Murphy!" Louder this time.

Sometimes the dog wandered through the gap between the

adjacent hangar and mine and roamed around the back grassy area. I peered that way, then I walked toward Hangar 3 to look around. A silhouette appeared around the side of a Pilatus. Tim, the charter mechanic waved.

"Murphy over there?"

Tim shook his head.

"Murph! Treat!"

I didn't have any treats on me, but I'd find one if he showed.

A sudden eruption of barking broke the silence. Distant, but frantic.

I sprinted across the grass at the far end of Hangar 4 and around the corner toward the shade hangars out back. The barks were mixed. Murphy, but a deeper snarl as well.

Shit.

I ran harder, my feet pounding across the asphalt taxiway and toward the sound. It was somewhere beyond the next hangar row but the noise echoed as it bounced from building to building.

A blur of fur streaked from around the corner of a hangar, Murphy, running like his tail was on fire, then another dog, bigger. Much bigger and coming after him like freight train. Had to be the dog from that damned Honda.

"Murphy!"

The blur that was my dog veered in my direction.

And that was my first mistake. Because the freight train turned too. It was muscular, big, some kind of Cane Corso Rottweiler mix. Had to be a hundred and twenty pounds minimum. Thank god Murphy was faster, but this dog looked determined to tear him to pieces.

And now he was headed for me.

I was completely unarmed, there was no sign of an owner for this beast, and it didn't show any indication of stopping.

Murphy slowed as he reached me, running past, but then circling around to defend me.

That was the last thing I wanted. At maybe seventy-five pounds, he wasn't small, but he was no match for this monster coming at us.

Murphy's fur was already matted and wet from previous contact, and this oncoming dog's mouth foamed in expectation of more. I didn't want to run, but standing in the middle of the taxiway was no kind of plan either.

The only things remotely passing for cover were the planes tied down in the shade hangars to my right.

I angled that way, still keeping my eyes on the Cane Corso. It came in fast, but paused to bark and snarl at me when I faced it. I was tall enough and big enough that maybe I warranted inspection before devouring. Murphy fanned out to one side, snarling and distracting the bigger dog, buying me time to move. I took the opportunity and sprinted for a Piper Saratoga in the nearest shade hangar. The low-wing aircraft was the only thing I could think of using for protection. The wing angled upward from about waist-high at the fuselage to almost chest high at the wing tip. The Cane Corso came after me hard.

I wasn't going to make it.

I leapt anyway, expecting to feel those big jaws clamp around my calf.

Murphy hit the Cane Corso in the side just as I got airborne, sending its bite wide and slamming the big dog into the Saratoga's nose gear. I rolled atop the aircraft's left wing, attempting to arrest my momentum. It was slippery up there. The wrong side of the plane to be climbing up. And now Murphy was in trouble, scrambling to avoid the snapping and biting of the Cane Corso's powerful jaws. Murphy yipped as the bigger dog's teeth grazed his flank and I shouted, screaming to get the attacking dog's attention. Murphy shot out and around the side of the Saratoga, not straying far from me, however.

"Murphy! Up!" I shouted.

The dog listened. He saw me up on the wing and made straight for me. Approaching the lower rear side of the wing like he'd done a thousand times, he readied himself to leap, but the Cane Corso exploded from under the wing and came flying up to hit Murphy just as he got airborne.

Both dogs hit the side of the empennage and went down in a mass of fur and snarling.

"Oh, Jesus," I blurted. Something halfway between a swear and a prayer. But then I was in motion. There was only one thing in reach even vaguely useful and that was a communication antenna angling back from the top of the plane. I seized it with both hands and snapped it off in one clean motion, then leapt down from the plane in a state of anger and stupidity I hadn't tried on in years.

The dogs were out of sight on the other side of the empennage so I hit the ground and rolled under the plane's tail, coming up to my feet again on the other side faster than I knew I was capable of.

The Cane Corso had Murphy down and was trying for a grip on the back of my scrambling dog's neck, and the first time I hit it with the communication antenna it didn't even notice. The dogs were both off balance already but the Cane Corso was planting its hind feet to get a better position. That was my next target. Forgoing the antenna attack, I grasped both of the dog's hind legs and hoisted them high. It was a dangerous move, like holding a tiger by the tail, but it was enough to force the dog to break its focus on Murphy and figure out how to get its feet back and attack me.

Murphy scrambled upright and came back for another attack, but I shouted to him again. "Murphy! Up!"

The dog looked confused for a moment. No doubt conflicted. "Up!"

This time he turned and found the plane access, then made

the leap onto the Saratoga's wing. The wing on this side was painted with tread grip near the fuselage, the normal walking path to the flight deck door, and he had no trouble keeping his footing. I had my hands full of snarling dog and no easy way out of my predicament, but if I could get a second of space I could survive. The dog was doing its best to kick loose of the death grip I had on its hind legs—but I didn't work out for nothing. I angled myself around, backing the dog up till I was as close to the Saratoga as I could get. My foot found the thin metal rod of the antenna on the ground and I kicked it closer to me, then I put all my force into my legs, pushing upward and throwing the dog over itself like I was dumping a wheelbarrow.

The big dog yelped and went rump over shoulders onto its back. I had time to snatch the antenna from the ground and scramble up onto the Saratoga's wing before the Cane Corso found its feet.

It came back warier, still furious, but with an edge of caution. Its gaze passed from Murphy to me before it set to barking. I had the antenna in front of me, waving it aggressively should it attempt to climb up.

Then came the whistle. High and loud. The dog immediately stopped barking to listen. The whistle chirped three times and the Cane Corso took off, sprinting for the sound. I turned to follow its path and there was a man at the end of its trajectory. He was muscular and hard-edged, dark complected with tattoos up his neck, though from this distance I couldn't make out what they were. He was in the intersection where I'd first spotted the dogs running and he stared across the taxiway at me. He pocketed his whistle.

His stance was casual, unapologetic. He had a cigarette in one hand and tucked it between his lips as the dog ran up. He took ahold of the big dog's collar and turned around with the beast, never giving me a second-glance. I felt in my pockets and found my phone, yanking it free and holding it up to snap a photo just before the pair disappeared around the corner of the hangar.

"What the hell," I muttered. "Assholes."

Murphy was panting at my side. The fur at his shoulder-blades was matted with blood.

I used the handle getting off the wing, then turned to help Murphy down. He made the leap but was favoring one leg when he walked.

"Come on, buddy. Let's get out of here."

We hurried toward my hangar.

A figure appeared in the pass-through between the hangars and I froze momentarily, but then Tim, the charter mechanic, stepped out.

"You okay, Luke? Heard all kinds of barking back here."

"Yeah," I muttered. I walked past him, shepherding Murphy along. "Big mean dog. Don't go that way."

"Oh shit," he said when he saw Murphy. "You need help?" His eyes lingered on the broken antenna I was still carrying.

"We'll be all right. Hold this." I handed him the antenna. "I'm going to get my gun."

I took Murphy upstairs and let him in my office, then stomped back down the stairs holding the Sig Sauer P365 I kept in my desk. My blood was still up stepping through the hangar door, but as I checked the load in the magazine, a female spoke from my left.

"Mister Angel, I'd recommend you put that down."

I turned to find a woman in a dark blue polo with the St. Pete Police logo on it. Her gun was drawn and she was aiming it at me.

FOURTEEN
SUSPECTED

"BIG PLANS FOR YOUR FRIDAY NIGHT?"

The gravity in Detective Blake Rivers' voice only lightened once I set my pistol on the ground.

"It's for protection. My dog was attacked."

Detective Rivers listened as I gave a brief accounting of the last few minutes, but it wasn't until Tim, the charter mechanic, saw the commotion and wandered back over to join us, that she finally holstered her weapon.

Even so, she watched carefully as I cleared the chamber on my Sig and stuffed the magazine in my back pocket.

"All kinds of excitement the last few days, eh, Luke?" Tim offered. "That engine-out landing last night, and then cops pulling guns on you today. You're like a regular James Bond."

Detective Rivers kept an indecipherable expression on her face as Tim expounded to her about my recent emergency landing. He had a tendency to exaggerate, but for once I was okay with it. He seemed to be establishing me as someone not in need of immediate shooting, and that struck me as important.

I kept my mouth shut till he was done and the detective

thanked him for his time. He gave me a sympathetic nod, and I returned a tight-lipped smile.

Once Tim had wandered back to his hangar, Detective Rivers followed me upstairs. I busied myself mending Murphy's wounds while she looked around my office.

"I'll have a patrol car swing by and check for anyone with a loose dog, or a Honda fitting the description you gave."

There was no reason to believe that the guy with the Cane Corso was going to linger after our altercation, but I muttered my thanks.

"We don't usually have animal problems out here. Just the occasional scuffle. Dogs being dogs. This was different. Aggressive."

She checked out a photo on my wall of me with Hank Martin. "You always keep a gun in your office?"

"Boy Scouts taught me to 'be prepared.'"

"Interesting. Didn't figure you enrolled as a Boy Scout. Had time for that between boosting airboats?"

I paused my efforts with Murphy and met her eye. "Someone's been digging."

"I'd be a piss-poor detective if I didn't. With a father like Frank Angel, currently serving fifteen years in Union. Brother Landon Angel with several warrants out for his arrest. When I saw the name Luke Angel come across my desk, I discovered it came with a colorful backstory." She moved over to my desk and had a look out the window.

"I was never convicted of any crimes, you'll notice. And the things you're talking about happened a long time ago."

"Innocence of youth defense?"

"Not claiming I was a teenaged Mother Theresa. But I distanced myself from my father and brother for a reason. Their current whereabouts don't concern me."

"Might concern *me*, if I find they are in the plane theft business."

"What would that have to do with me?"

"I don't know. Here I am investigating a missing person and a missing aircraft. Turns out the last person to see them alive is named Angel and has a family history involving plane theft. Could be coincidence. But you have to admit it's curious."

Detective Rivers took a seat in one of my client chairs and slouched against the armrests. She had a confidence about her that was undeniable. I was bigger than her, a possible physical threat, even without my gun, but she looked as relaxed as a lioness. Possibly as dangerous.

"Chris Carter's disappearance doesn't have anything to do with my family."

"Good to hear. Because I did research into the last known activity of Landon Angel and there is some indication that he might have picked up where your daddy left off. Suspicion of drug smuggling, possibly guns. Hard to say what he's been up to. But it seems he's still flying around somewhere."

"If I see him, I can let you know. But I won't be seeing him."

"You should know, the lab techs found a fair amount of blood in the hangar you opened up for us. The one belonging to Dr. Carter. We're still working to determine the source, seems like someone mopped it up with aviation fuel which made things difficult, but we're now investigating the possibility of foul play."

Blood.

And an answer to why the hangar had smelled so strongly of avgas.

"Ava said she found a suicide note on Chris's phone."

"That's true. A typed note, which is interesting, because it could have been written by anyone. Also interesting is Dr. Carter's lack of a medical history of depression or mental illness."

"They don't let pilots with mental illness keep medical

certificates. Could be lots of reasons he might have failed to report something like that."

"True. We're certainly not done investigating the possibility of suicide. But we're keeping our options open. Right now, locating Dr. Carter is our top priority."

I finished looking Murphy over and moved toward my desk. "So how can I help you, detective?"

She appraised me with one eyebrow arched. "You can make yourself available. We may have some questions regarding aspects of your relationship with Dr. Carter's family. Your ex-wife was kind enough to provide us with some recent financial statements for your shared business, but it's possible we may require more."

"Records for Archangel? Why would you need those?"

"It's a routine part of the investigation. We like to have a complete picture. I noticed your business carries a lot of debt. Is that typical?"

I frowned at her. Archangel's finances being put under a microscope hadn't been part of my evening's plans.

"Holding debt is a normal part of aircraft ownership. There's a lot of overhead to this business."

"And I understand, you've also been dealing with some partnership concerns. Your former father-law is a business partner."

She'd been a busy woman.

This conversation felt like taking a checkride I'd failed to study for.

"Archangel is a healthy business. I pay my bills. My partners and I work things out in-house. I fail to see what any of this has to do with Chris."

Detective Rivers knit her fingers in her lap. "There are only a few constants in my line of work. But when we encounter a crime, it nearly always comes down to money. Though sometimes it's sex. Do you mind if I ask what your relationship with Mrs. Carter is like?"

Her eye contact didn't waver. Maybe that was something they taught in cop school.

The question about Ava didn't sound spontaneous. She was fishing for something.

"I think I'd like to get on with my evening. It's been a day and my dog needs attention."

"I understand." She rose. "I'm going to give you my card. I have your phone number already. If you get to thinking about anything you want to share with me, you can give me a call. Okay?"

"Don't be offended if I don't see you out."

"I can find the door myself. I'll be nearby, Mr. Angel. And I'm sure I'll see you soon."

She closed the door lightly behind her.

I waited till her footfalls had made it all the way to the ground floor and the pedestrian hangar door had slammed shut before I let out my swears.

The parking lot for Demens Landing marina was quiet when I made it home. The way I liked it. I checked my mailbox on the way in. The second I opened the door, a slip of paper fell out. No envelope. It was crumpled and folded, like it had been forcibly crammed into the edge of the box. I picked it up and deciphered the nearly illegible scrawl. It was a phone number and the word "Call."

What kind of bullshit was this?

I gathered the rest of my junk mail and dumped it in the neighboring trash can, but kept the slip with the number on it as I walked to the boat.

I was tired. Running away from dogs and becoming a murder

suspect was exhausting work. But when I finally made it aboard the *Midlife Crisis* and put Murphy inside, I took a seat in my thinking chair and pulled out my phone. No calls from Cassidy. Marie had texted a photo of a cocktail she was having somewhere. The siren's call of easy living.

If I was any kind of smart, I'd ditch anything to do with the Carters, go find Marie, and have a carefree night of drinks and clothing-optional entertainment. It was an alluring thought.

I considered the crumpled slip of paper with the handwritten number on it.

Did I want to know who was on the other end? Probably not.

But getting to sleep tonight was going to be hard enough without something like this hanging over my head.

I dialed the number.

Three rings, then the voice spoke.

"Hey, little brother. It's about time we talked."

Turns out I wasn't any kind of smart.

FIFTEEN

LANDON

I DIDN'T HAVE a clear image in my head of the last time I'd heard my brother's voice. A voicemail after my wedding maybe. He sounded older now, the timbre of his speech more like that of my father than I recalled.

"In case you were wondering, there's a possibility this phone is tapped," I said. "If it's not, it might be once the local PD gets a warrant. Hang up now if you feel like it."

"Getting yourself into trouble with the cops? Seems unlike you."

"Nobody saw anything. Wasn't that always your defense?"

"Let's not talk about me. Called about you."

"Um hm. Sure. And why is that?" I considered the twilight sky above me.

"Can't a big brother check in on his family? That's my job. Looking out for you."

"Dawning revelation you've had tonight? Where was that in our youth?"

"I recall taking plenty of heat for you. Remember the Farley brothers? They both got black eyes when they messed with you."

"After the fact. Taking a sock full of golf balls to their faces while they slept didn't help me when they were kicking my ass behind the Stop 'n Shop."

"Never did it again though, did they?"

"What do you want, Landon?"

"Well, that's a complicated question."

"Un-complicate it for me."

He fidgeted with something on the other end. Papers maybe. "You remember dad's seaplane stories? All the places he went, adventures he had even before we were born?"

"Pretty sure half of those were made up."

"He did have a way of exaggerating. Something I only realized the usefulness of when I got older."

"Couldn't exaggerate his way out of prison."

"Maybe not. But the older I got, the more I've wondered which parts of the stories resembled truth more than fiction. Sometimes there's a good reason to lead people off-target."

"If there's a point to this story, you'd best find it soon. I've had a long day."

"I'm unearthing buried treasure, brother. A thing we thought lost. And I wanted you to know I found it."

Water lapped the edges of the *Midlife Crisis* while I absorbed his words.

"There's no treasure of his I want."

"That's a lie. There's one. And that's what I've got my hands on. A jungle resurrection story is happening."

"Where?"

"I'm keeping the details quiet."

"Then why call me?"

"Because things are getting complicated. The person who has what we need to reclaim our treasure doesn't deal in cash as much as favors. I've been trying to do her a solid, but there's been a snag. I could use your help unsnagging it."

"Why would I?"

"You know why. You want to see this piece of family history come home as much as I do."

"You owe this person?"

"It's on her land. I've involved her people. So yeah, I've got obligations. And she's not someone you walk out on easily."

"Sounds like you. Finding the worst people you can to do business with."

"She'll play fair when it benefits her."

"What a ringing endorsement."

"I've had a guy in your area. Your paths might have crossed. He was doing some work for us, but isn't making the headway we'd hoped. Could use someone with your skills."

"Why don't *you* handle it?"

"I'm not local. She's keeping me close by. But I'm about ready to cut loose and fly into the sunset. All I need is this deal for her resolved, then we're home free."

"Stop saying we. I haven't agreed to anything."

"But you will, brother. I know you will. It's what you do, you fly to the rescue. Don't tell me you don't have the medals to prove it. I've kept up."

"I'm not in the business of cleaning up your messes. I've got a life here. Things are going just fine without you."

Mostly.

"Think about it, Luke. You know what we could do together."

"No. I don't want the strings it comes with. I've listened long enough. Whatever it is you're planning, you're on your own."

"Bro."

"Don't bro me. You've lost the privilege."

I hung up.

Same Landon.

This was exactly what Dad would do. Dig himself into some hole and then bury the entire family with him. I wasn't falling for it. Not again. I stuffed my phone in my pocket and went inside.

I inspected Murphy's wounds a second time. His head was on my lap as I camped on the couch in the main living area. His breathing was quiet and by the grace of God he'd sustained only minor injuries. He'd been gouged along his back and again on his rear leg, but the wounds weren't deep and while he might carry a couple of scars, he'd come out healthy enough. Things could have been a lot worse.

Recalling the attack made me livid.

There were plenty of dogs at the airport on any given day. Owners showed up with them frequently, and the flight school hosted a pair of lovable mutts that came to work with the manager. Murphy had made friends with all of them over the years. Roughhousing wasn't uncommon. They were dogs. But nothing had ever approached the scale of the Cane Corso's attack.

I pulled out my phone and checked the photo of the asshole owner I'd taken, zooming in as much as I could manage. It was a bad angle, only showing the guy's back. Black jeans, and white T-shirt, shaved head, tattoos up his neck onto the back of his skull and down both arms. Not much to go on. But there was something familiar about the look. I'd seen his type before.

Once the army relaxed rules on tattoos there had been plenty of guys that covered everything they were allowed to with ink, but this guy was hitting farther back in my memory bank. The kind of guys who used to hang around my father in my youth.

Maybe it was just the call from my brother dredging up old memories.

Growing up in Central Florida you met all types, but my dad's business had attracted some of the least desirable factions of the population. Frank Angel had a reputation for being a man who delivered. His ability to fly and a lax attitude toward laws and regulations had made him a useful friend for people with goods to move and restrictions to avoid. For a long time I'd thought it was cool. Like he was Han Solo, a rogue hero, blasting off to exotic destinations and coming home with treasures and a princess.

Parts of him had even lived up to the legend. But the princess he'd brought home from a distant land had left home to escape a life of violence, not start a new one. My mother was a Mexican beauty who had fallen for Frank Angel's cocky swagger. The surfer dude from Florida with a plane and ticket to paradise. They'd met on a beach in Tulum and he'd hooked her on his airborne lifestyle.

From all accounts, it must have been ideal for awhile. Soaring around the Caribbean, jaunts from the Keys to the Carolina coast. Belize. Colombia. With his small fleet of Piper Aztecs and a Grumman Mallard he'd named after my mother, Frank Angel had been the lord of the sky. Until US Customs and the Organized Crime Drug Enforcement Task Force came calling. Then it was stress and fear and constant moving. And the big lie.

I moved Murphy off my lap and climbed off the couch—too many unwelcome memories surfacing. I had to shift, find my way back to the bow. I poured myself a glass of bourbon on the way, then I took a seat in my old deck chair and took in the evening sky. The bow was facing east. The moon rose amber above the horizon, nearly full.

The sky behind me changed colors. Sunset on a day that hadn't gone anything like I'd expected. I certainly hadn't made any progress on finding Chris. And now I was a suspect in his disappearance. Rivers had said foul play. Blood hastily wiped up. I swirled the bourbon in my glass and sipped it and sat with the reality that my friend was likely dead. Possibly murdered?

By my second drink, stars and planets appeared. Pegasus.

Jupiter. The Great Bear. All the familiar old gods hung in the firmament. Silent judges.

Frank Angel had taught Landon and me the locations of the constellations. I didn't realize at the time that his celestial navigation abilities had served him well on low flights around the Keys with his lights and avionics off.

It had been my mother who taught me the stories behind the stars, some I was pretty sure she made up, but I hadn't heard her voice telling them in a long time.

There were nights that she came to mind more often than others. The nights I wondered what life would have been like had she lived. Nothing in the sky ever gave me the answer to that question, but it seemed a large enough repository for my wondering. On occasion I'd wonder if Frank Angel was able to see the same stars I could from his cell in the Union Correctional Institution.

I hoped not.

SIXTEEN

DIRT ROAD

I KNOCKED on the door of Reese's house in Kenwood around seven-thirty in the morning.

Not a great hour to be showing up unannounced on a Saturday. Felt worse about it when Reese wasn't the one to open the door. The young woman wore a long T-shirt that made it to mid-thigh and wooly socks. She was pretty, even in her morning state, with long tangled black hair hanging past her shoulders.

"Hey, I'm sorry. I was looking for Reese." I had a grip on Murphy's collar to keep him from charging straight in. "Sorry if I woke you."

"You didn't. Just making coffee. Reese is still asleep though. You must be Luke."

"I am. Sorry. I don't recall meeting you."

"You haven't. Met your dog though. Hey, Murphy."

The dog's tail was going a mile a minute so I let him go. He immediately leapt at the chance to nuzzle her hand. She opened the door a little wider. Want to come in?"

"I was hoping I could trouble Reese to watch Murphy for a

few hours this morning, but I don't want to impose if you two have plans."

"No big plans. Just a lazy Saturday. Want a cup of coffee? I'm making an Americano. I can fix you one." She headed for a shiny espresso machine on the kitchen counter.

I stepped in the doorway a few feet. The place looked fresher than the last time I'd seen it. New stuff, like the espresso machine, but better organized somehow. Some new art.

"Reese been redecorating?"

The woman at the coffee-maker looked around the room then bit her lip before responding. "She didn't tell you, did she." My confusion must have been evident, because she continued. "I moved in a few weeks ago."

"Ah. Congratulations." I scratched at the back of my neck. "She's always been private."

We looked at each other across the kitchen island and she nodded. "I like that about her."

"Me too. Sounds like I should probably know your name though."

She smiled and slid the paper to-go cup of espresso toward me. "Kara." She had kind brown eyes, the type that make you feel seen. "Does Murphy need food? I saw we have a bag in the closet."

"I hope to be back by lunchtime. He probably won't eat again till tonight. Got in a fight last night though. Maybe let him take it easy? Otherwise I'd take him with me."

"Aw, poor baby. Luckily all our Saturday plans involve couches."

"I appreciate you doing this. Oh, one other thing. When Reese is up, will you ask her if she wants to join me at the range later?"

"The . . . shooting range?"

"Just getting in some practice. No worries if she can't go."

"All right. I'll ask her." Kara had lost her smile.

"Thanks." I held up the coffee cup. "For this too."

I handed my phone to Tyson as soon as I got to the airport. "You know anything about enhancing photographs?" I was feeling the caffeine from the Americano. Ready to make things happen.

He took the phone and gave me the look young people always gave me when I asked a tech question. "Like zooming?"

"I know how to zoom in. I'm not an idiot. I was just wondering if you knew any ways to sharpen an image and give me some clarity. Don't they have a bunch of social media filters and shit for that these days?"

"Oh. All right. Maybe. I've got a photo editing app might work. You mean like the contrast and color and stuff?"

"Whatever makes it easier to get some details."

"Enhance. You're being all CSI or some shit. Just email it to me. It's easier." He handed the phone back.

I found the photo for him and emailed it. We were outside the hangar ready to preflight the Cessna 185 we used for tailwheel instruction. The old plane belonged to a customer, but we'd worked out a maintenance deal for Tyson to get some time in it.

It was Saturday morning so the ramp had a weekend vibe. More flight students, fewer mechanics.

Rip waved hello on his way to give rides in a Stearman biplane. The old WWII trainer dated to the forties and always added an air of vintage nostalgia to the morning.

Bannerland was already diving their old planes at the runway, picking up advertisements to haul out to the beach, and The Hangar restaurant was doing a booming brunch business.

I finished preflighting around the time Tyson finished with his phone. "There. Check your email again. Best I can do."

I opened the image and he had indeed sharpened it significantly. The cropped image was now almost entirely the tattooed man with a slice of the Cane Corso in the frame. The details of the man stood out better, including the tattoos up the back of his arms and neck. One caught my attention immediately, a modified take on a tiger, except with square angles and an exaggerated expression.

"You see anything useful?" Tyson asked.

"Maybe. Guy's likely prison gang affiliated."

"Oh shit. How you know?"

I zoomed in on the image of the cat symbol and showed it to him.

He wrinkled his brow. "Looks like it belongs on a pyramid or something."

"Not far off. I think it's Mayan."

"Mexico? They have tigers?"

"Not the real thing. But there's a gang called Los Tigres Yucatan. Reminds me of something they'd use."

"What would a Mexican gang member be doing here at Whitted?"

"That's what I want to know." I checked the scattered clouds above us. "Let's get in the air, anyway. I'll worry about this later."

We climbed in and Tyson did an admirable job of picking up where we'd left off on his last lesson. Tailwheel checkouts weren't as intensive as learning to fly in the first place, but it took a delicate touch to get right if all you've ever flown are tricycle gear aircraft. We bobbed our way to Runway 7 and took off southeast, making our way across the bay toward a grass strip called Manatee. Tyson bounced it a few times on the landing and needed a bit of advice, but the next time around greased it in for a clean three-point landing. I tried to keep my thoughts on the lesson, but my mind kept wandering back to the Cane Corso attack and the guy with the tattoos.

On climb-out I pointed east. "Go that way. I've got another spot I want to have you try."

Tyson followed my instructions and headed east. It took the better part of twenty minutes of cruising, and I could tell Tyson was itching to get to more landings, but I kept him busy searching out the window for the strip when we got close.

"You sure there's an airport out here? I don't see anything on the chart."

"Doesn't always have to be on a chart to be a good airstrip."

I finally spotted the privately owned length of field I was hunting for. To the uninitiated, it just looked like more farmland, and that's essentially what it was. But if you looked closely enough, you could spot a tattered wind sock near a long stretch of dirt road.

It would be narrow for someone of Tyson's skill level, but you had to learn somehow.

"That's it. Set us up and put it down just past that stand of trees."

Tyson gave me a reluctant nod and eased back on the throttle.

I kept an eye on the farmhouse as we flew the downwind leg. A pair of horses were grazing in a pasture out back. A dog appeared from under a tree and started barking. Couldn't hear it, but it looked enthusiastic about it.

Tyson's control coming down was excellent. Used all forty degrees of flaps and had us on an excellent glide path for final approach.

"Short-field procedure," I reminded him, and he bled off a little more airspeed.

"This is super skinny, man. You sure we can land here?"

"We'll find out soon, won't we."

He flared the plane a few feet over the dirt road and held it off.

"Good, good, let it settle." We touched down and the wheels made a gratifying crunching sound as we rolled along. "Level, level and . . . There we go," I said as the tailwheel finally touched down. "Just keep us straight."

"Where the hell we go now? No taxiway."

I glanced at the farmhouse out the left window. The dog had torn out of the yard and was cutting across the field to intercept us. I placed a hand on the mixture control, ready to cut the engine if it got too close, but this wasn't the dog's first encounter with an airplane, and it wisely kept its distance, barking at us from the other side of a split rail fence.

Our wing was high enough to clear a mailbox as we taxied off the road.

"My controls," I said, and Tyson released his grip on the throttle.

I kicked the left rudder pedal and turned the plane off the road and headed toward the farm house.

"Luke, this is just someone's driveway now."

"I know."

"You know these people?"

"Used to."

He straightened in his seat. "Oh shit, dude."

A woman in a floral muumuu had walked out onto the porch of the farmhouse. She was holding a shotgun. She hoisted it to her shoulder and aimed.

SEVENTEEN
BE COOL

"JUST BE COOL," I said.

I'd pulled the mixture control out and popped the door open on the high-wing Cessna. The woman on the porch was keeping a steady bead on the plane with her shotgun while the engine quit.

I climbed out. "You can stay in the plane if you want."

Tyson made a noise that sounded like "Pffht." I took it to mean he hadn't considered doing anything else.

"I'll be back in a bit."

The side of the plane had shielded me from the porch, but when I came around the nose, I had my hands up.

"Hey there."

The barking dog was an angry mutt with a broad chest, but it didn't get close.

"Brisco, shut it!" the woman on the porch shouted.

The dog gave one last bark for good measure, but then settled down to a low grumble.

"Hey, Margery. It's Luke."

The old woman squinted. "Luke Angel? Can't be."

"Against all odds."

She lowered the shotgun. "Well, shit. You know better than to roll up on a woman with eyes bad as mine."

"Sweet as you are, I was never in any real danger."

She laughed. "Sweet. Hah. You haven't changed a lick, have you."

"Just older and slower."

"Ain't that the way it goes. Well, all right. Come on up here. Who's that you got in the plane?"

"Flight student. Teaching him where real pilots land. He's going to stay in the plane. I won't bother you long."

"You aren't a bother yet. I'll let you know when you are. Come let me have a look at you."

I approached slowly, tossing a dog biscuit to the mutt along the way. His disposition improved immediately.

Margery Wagner had never been a slender woman, almost as wide as she was tall, but she had a pleasantly round face and a voice that carried across hills. Her hair was shorter now, grayer too, but I caught a whiff of the perfume she wore and took me straight back to my childhood.

"Gawd, it's been a long time." She waddled to the steps to have a better view of me. With me on the ground and her on the porch, we were about the same height. She propped the shotgun on the porch railing. "All right, get up here."

I climbed the steps and she wrapped me in a bosomy hug.

"You're too skinny. You must still be single. Why aren't you married yet?"

"Tried it. Didn't stick."

"My invitation got lost in the mail, I bet."

"We eloped. Cheaper."

"Shame. You would have looked good in a tux." She patted my back. "You hungry?"

"I don't want to take up your whole morning. And my student is terrified."

"Of Brisco? That useless dog couldn't catch a rabbit with a peg leg. Makes a lot of noise is all he does." She gestured to the dog. "Brisco, get up here." The dog meandered back onto the porch.

"How's Earl?"

"Oh, right as rain." The answer came too quick.

"Bad?"

"He likes to complain about my nursing abilities. Don't listen to him. Lives like a king up there."

"I'd like to see him."

She sighed. "I'd best check on him first, but come in."

We entered through the screen door and the smell of the place hit me first. Baked goods and potpourri, furniture polish, and the lingering scent of nicotine. The place hadn't changed much in twenty years. The same fat ceramic bear held its tummy on the kitchen table. Margery caught me looking. "Been a while since I kept your favorite cookies in the house. You and your brother used to get in that jar like raccoons."

"You heard anything from him?"

"Let me get upstairs and tell Earl it's you. He'd a heard the plane and might be worrying. We'll talk more after."

The way she'd dodged the question hadn't escaped me, but I didn't press her as she made her way to the steps and took a firm grip on the railing before hoisting herself up.

I surveyed the living room's assortment of knickknacks and browsed the old picture frames. Earl had an eight point buck head mounted on the wall, along with a jackalope my childhood self had been convinced was real for far longer than I liked to admit.

In one corner of the room hung a framed photo of Earl in the 1980s, standing alongside my father. The pair were posing in front of a 1947 Grumman Mallard—my father's most classic plane, *Tropic Angel*. Stuck in the corner of the frame was a faded Polaroid showing my older brother Landon and me posing in the same positions as Frank and Earl. Landon had his arm around my shoulder and stood about three inches taller. I looked about seven.

That plane. How many times had Landon and I sat at those controls and imagined future adventures in it? That cockpit had been our fortress, our church. I could still smell it.

Landon's words on the phone came back to me. "A jungle resurrection story is happening."

Lost treasure.

"You can come on up now, Luke."

I set the Polaroid back against the frame, then headed up the stairs.

The smells changed around the hallway. Disinfectant and the sour scent of illness hung in the air like carrion birds.

Margery stood at one side of the doorway to the bedroom as sentry. I was obligated to squeeze past her to enter.

Earl was in a mechanical hospital bed, adjusted so he was sitting up about forty-five degrees. His beard was long, but clean. His eyes were glassy.

"Hey, old man," I said.

"The prodigal son returns," Earl said. "Your shoulders got bigger. You one of them gym rats?"

"I lift the occasional large object from time to time. Surfboards count?"

"I remember those days. Costa Rica once. That was a good time."

"You look good."

"Like hell I do. Look like a cancer sandwich. 'Bout what I am these days too."

"You're too cranky and stubborn to get sick. I don't buy it."

There was a folding chair near the bed so I eased myself into it. Margery had disappeared.

"You remembered how to land here. That's something."

"I need to bring you a new wind sock."

"What did you fly in? Sounded like a six-cylinder."

"Cessna one-eighty-five with an IO-550 Continental."

"Nice bird."

"It's no Decathlon. You taught me tailwheels should come with a stick, not a yoke."

"I'd take anything with wings these days. They're all good."

"Don't have it anymore?"

"Nah. Went with all the other shit worth anything around here. Damned medical bills. Shoulda took that plane up to Alaska and let a bear eat me years ago. Too late now."

"Call me when you're ready. I'll bring you a Florida panther."

Earl laughed, then it turned into a cough and a wince.

"Getting old sucks," he muttered. "I don't recommend it."

"Can I get you anything?"

"Just tell me what you're here for so I can get on with dying in peace."

I leaned forward and rested an elbow on the bed. "Ran into somebody at Whitted last night. An asshole with a mean dog. Had a tigres tattoo."

"And?"

"And I need to know if it's got anything to do with Dad. Or Landon."

Earl sniffed and looked out the window.

"If there was anyone outside that Frank would confide in, it would be you. And this guy reminds me of the kind of guys that used to come sniffing around back in the day. Made me suspicious."

"Your daddy was no gang member."

"Knew some though. Flew shit for people."

"Flew for damned near everybody."

"And Landon?"

"Couldn't say anything about what he's up to."

"Tell me there's no connection, I'll believe you, but I just need to make sure nothing from Frank's dealings are leaking over to Whitted."

"You're worried about your airport? Your dad's been out of business for decades. He's in prison for God's sake."

"Doesn't mean business stopped. Kind of guys he knew back then didn't suddenly run out of motivation."

"Whatever your daddy is up to, you should probably ask him."

Like hell if that was going to happen.

Earl was frowning.

I located his knee under the sheets and rested a hand on it. "I didn't know you were this sick. I would've come sooner."

"Nobody needs to worry themselves about me."

"Earl, I want you to know something true. I didn't run away from you back in the day. You or Aunt Margie. You two were about as close to family as it gets. My leaving wasn't ever to do with you."

"When you did your bit in the Army, we were all proud of you. We knew you had to figure some things out." Earl shifted in the bed. "There's days I wonder how things could'a gone had your mama lived and Frank didn't get himself busted. Those were some grand days we had back when they were together. Still miss those enchiladas your mama used to make. God, what I wouldn't give for some of those now. But Frank was always gonna be Frank. None of it was meant to last. We had a good run though."

"As far as I'm concerned, Frank's right where he belongs. But if any of this business I'm getting a whiff of over in Saint Pete even vaguely smells of him, he's going to wish I didn't know where they had him."

"If I hear from him, you want me to pass that on? That it?"

"You can tell him I came to see you. But he shouldn't hold his breath for the same consideration." I pushed off the chair and stood. "I'll let you get your rest." I moved toward the door.

"Luke?"

"Yeah."

He was looking back out the window. "This seems like maybe it's one of those conversations you have when you're not sure there's going to be another one. So I'd best say what needs saying."

I waited.

"I always knew the truth about what happened with your mama, but I never said nothing to the cops. Still think about that sometimes." He looked me in the eye now.

"Wouldn't have changed anything."

"Me and Margie didn't want to see you boys lose both parents at once. Frank did the best he could for you after."

"No. He didn't. But I don't blame you. You were a better father to your kids than Frank ever was to me."

I moved through the door but Earl spoke again.

"Your daddy did call us not long ago."

I paused.

"Asked Margie to dig something out of the barn and mail it to your brother."

"What was it?"

"Some of his old flying stuff. From his time down in Mexico. Useless, seemed like. But we sent it."

I chewed my cheek. "All right. Thanks, I guess. Where did he have her send it?"

"Down to the Keys. Marathon."

"So Landon was back in Florida."

"Long enough to pick up mail anyway. Not that anyone ever could pin that boy down. You and him was born pilots. Not a place in this wide world big enough to hold you."

"Might be because Landon never found a place that would let him stick around long before having to arrest him. Just like Dad."

"You see him, you might still have a few things in common."

"Won't be seeing him if I can help it."

Earl was back to looking out the window when I shut the door.

EIGHTEEN
NO CONTACT

TYSON WAS STANDING in the living room when I made it back downstairs.

"Thought you were going to wait in the plane."

"Had to pee."

Margery emerged from the kitchen. "Found your friend here fixing to urinate on my hydrangeas. Told him to come inside."

She had a plate with vanilla cookies on it and offered me one.

"I'm good, thanks."

Tyson went for a couple. "You never told me your family flew too." He pointed to the photograph of me with the seaplane. "She says your dad had that sweet flying boat. What happened to it?"

"Gone with the rest of my dad's poor decisions. Crashed in a jungle somewhere supposedly."

"That was a grand old plane," Margery said. "Not many like them, and none as pretty as that one. Frank even named it for Luke's mama."

"And lost it because he's a lying criminal," I added.

"Sounds like you got a few issues with your dad, huh?" Tyson said, munching his cookie.

"No issue. As long as he stays in prison. Margie, Earl said Frank had you mail something to Landon in the Keys. You have that address for me?"

Margery frowned. "It was just one of those letter drop places. Like a post office box."

"What else of Frank's do you have here?"

"Not much. Just a few things in the barn he wanted us to hold on to while he was gone."

"What did Landon want with it?"

"No idea. Your daddy asked to send a few things and we did. Just old maintenance manuals mostly."

"What for?"

"For the Mallard."

"Why not email it?" Tyson added. "Isn't everything online now anyway?"

"Some restoration projects are harder than others," I muttered.

"I suppose if you really want to know more about it, you'll have to ask your dad," Margery said.

Not likely.

"I appreciate your hospitality. We're taking off."

"You mind if I get one more of those?" Tyson snagged a last cookie on the way out.

Descending the front steps, I looked north toward the old barn that had doubled as an aircraft hangar for many years. The scene brought back more memories. I'd learned to fly all over Central Florida, but this had been a common destination throughout my childhood. I'd done my first aerobatics in Earl's Decathlon when I was no more than ten. I found myself wandering over to the barn without much in the way of thought.

The big doors were closed but not locked. I slid one open a crack and peered inside.

The dusty interior space held tack for the horses and a few

farming vehicles. Still had enough room for a plane too, but the spot the Decathlon had maintained for decades was vacant.

Old bins were stacked in a pile near the stairs to the hayloft. Most of it was Earl's but I spotted several dry-rotting rubbermaid containers with my dad's handwriting on them in faded Sharpie.

I went to the bins and considered them a moment before popping the lid off one and browsing through the contents.

Tyson had followed me into the barn.

"This place have all kinds of nostalgia for you?" He eyed a banner hanging from the ceiling that advertised a long-forgotten airshow.

I dug through some ancient headsets and yellowed flight manuals and came up with a survival knife in a sheath. It was the type with a compartment in the handle that held matches and fishing line and had a compass on the sheath. The blade of the knife was rusty but the compass still worked.

"What are you looking for?" Tyson asked.

"I don't know. Nothing."

"Should be easy to find."

"Yeah." I tossed the knife back into the bin and moved on to another. "I don't get why Frank is suddenly digging up his old gear for Landon."

"You asking like you want an answer or are you being all rhetorical?"

"It doesn't matter." I was about to close the lid on the second bin, but the corner of a photograph caught my eye. It was jutting out from one of the private pilot aviation test guides. A bit of color against the black and white. I tugged at the photo and it came loose.

It was Mom.

She was in a sundress, laughing near the edge of Lake Okeechobee.

It was a unique shot from low angle, taken by a child perhaps.

Had to be early on. She had none of the sadness in her eyes. She looked happy. I'd never seen the photo before but it was familiar. The lakeside. She'd always gone to the water for solace. *Tropic Angel* sat in the background. Like she was posing with it.

"Who's that looker?" Tyson asked. "She's a hottie."

"You always this nosy?"

"Only when you bring me on a tour of BFE for a flight lesson."

"She's my mom."

"Oh. Shit. She's dead though, right?"

I sighed. "Yeah."

"How'd she die?"

I closed the lid on the bin but kept the photograph. "None of your business."

"It's obvious this place is like the Luke Angel childhood trauma zone or something. Way you moping around. Figured I might as well know why."

"I'm not moping."

"My bad. You're a ray of sunshine. Got Auntie Shotgun up there on the porch, bin of history out here. You looking at pictures of your smokeshow mom from the sixties or something. Real fun times."

"It wasn't the sixties. How old do you think I am?"

"I don't know, man. Forty?"

"They don't teach enough math in school anymore."

"Couple of my lifetimes ago no matter how you add it."

He wasn't wrong there.

"Let's go," I said, heading for the door.

"My cousin had his mom die when he was little. He's doing fine. I don't think he spends much time in barns or anything. She only died from a heart problem though. Wasn't polio like yours."

I stared at Tyson and shook my head. "You're failing your flight lesson."

"Typhoid? That was an olden days disease, right?"

"She died in plane crash. You happy now?"

"Oh. That sucks."

"It did, in fact, suck. Thanks for your insightful analysis."

We made it back to the plane and got it turned around, then climbed in. I thought I'd gotten some peace from Tyson, but as soon as we had headsets on and the intercom powered up, he was back at it.

"So way I see it is you got all this angst about your mom because she was like the real parent and your dad was kind of a deadbeat, is that it? Though he had that cool plane so he must have been doing something right."

"I've decided my rates for flight instruction are going up after this lesson. Don't make me unplug your headset."

"I'm serious though. You really hate your dad that bad? My dad was kind of a deadbeat too. Ran out on my mom to go be with my stepmom. I mean, I guess she's my stepmom now, but I don't really call her mom or anything. I still got my real mom, though. I think what my dad did was messed up, but I don't know if I *hate* him."

He primed the engine with the fuel pump. Then he waited. He was too damned sincere. The innocence of youth.

"You know what? I'm going to tell you the truth and you're going to tell zero other people, and then you're going to be radio silent for the ride back except for actual flying conversation, you get me?"

"Fair."

"Good. When the plane went down, my parents were both in it. But Frank got out and left my mom in there because he'd also stashed a bunch of cocaine in the back and didn't want to get caught with it. So when the police showed up they only found my mom at the controls. Frank denied all association with the flight and said my mom was the one doing the smuggling. The woman had barely earned a private license, but he claimed she was acting solo. What's worse is the police said that when they showed up, she was still alive. But she died before the ambulance arrived. If my chickenshit father had gotten her medical attention right away, she might have lived."

"Damn. Thats's messed up."

"That's why Frank Angel can rot in hell."

"I was right about the childhood trauma thing, huh?"

"Everyone has their issues. If you can get through life not hating your dad, then great. I'm happy for you. Just not the way my story went." I cranked the engine and it roared to life.

Tyson adjusted his mic. "Kinda surprised you turned out so normal. You're still probably the coolest dude I know that's like middle-aged or whatever."

"I'm thirty-six."

He nodded. "That's what I'm saying."

I taxied the airplane toward the road. "I'll tell you another secret. When you get to be my age, you don't miss being your age."

"Because you're losing your memory already? That's sad."

And I laughed.

The kid was a smartass.

Made sense why I still liked him. Reminded me of me.

NINETEEN

ON CAMERA

I WAS STANDING IN REESE WINTERS' living room, retrieving my dog, when a text from Detective Rivers came through. It had a video attachment.

The text read:

>>> Care to comment?

I tapped the black-and-white video image and watched it play. It was a three second surveillance video of a hotel hallway. The clip showed Ava Carter kissing me.

"What the shit," I muttered.

"You look like someone just pissed in your fuel tanks," Reese said. She was seated at a stool near the kitchen counter.

I watched the video one more time and slid it across to her. "Someone has to be messing with me."

"Oh damn. Is that Ava Carter?"

Reese's partner Kara leaned over her shoulder to watch as well.

"That's from a vacation we all took years ago. Ava got drunk one night and came onto me in a hotel hallway."

"Yeesh," Kara said. "This was while you were still married to her sister?"

"Yeah."

"Does Cassidy know?" Reese asked.

"I never told her."

Both women looked at me with raised eyebrows.

"Hey, this video doesn't show it, but two seconds after this I pushed her into her hotel room and shut her in there. She was drunk. She was going through a rough time with Chris. Me and Cass already had enough issues at the time. I was trying to preserve my marriage, not end it. I wasn't about to lob that grenade into the mix."

"Ava never said anything about it either?"

"I wasn't sure Ava remembered it happening. Next day she was hungover as all hell, never said a word. I let it go. Kept my distance ever since."

"Who's this Blake Rivers person?" Reese asked, checking the contact info.

I gave her a rundown of my meeting with the detective.

"Damn. With Chris gone? You know this makes you look bad, right?"

"Chris? The pilot guy who went missing?" Kara tagged in. "I thought that was suicide."

"I told Kara about it," Reese said with a shrug.

I waved the comment away and collected my phone. The video glared back at me.

This was a tactic. Detective Rivers' question about Ava in my office had been fishing for this. She'd probably already seen the video then. She just wanted to see if I came clean.

"She's going to put this down as motive," I muttered. "She thinks Chris was murdered."

"Whoa," Kara said.

I filled them in on the detective's claims of finding blood in the hangar.

"So Saint Pete Police are looking at this as homicide and she sends you this. How would she come up with this video? Who else knew about it?"

"Had to be Ava. Rivers asked about my relationship with her and I blew the question off."

"Looks like Ava didn't," Reese said.

I picked up Murphy's leash. "I need to talk to Cassidy."

"You think she's seen it?"

"I don't know. But if not, I want her to hear it from me. Things are already tense with Archangel. Last thing I need is her to have more excuses to bail."

Kara gave me a sympathetic smile that was anything but reassuring. I used my phone and called Cassidy. It rang several times then went to voicemail.

"Damn it," I muttered, then scrolled up on Cassidy's contact info. I tapped her profile pic and her location popped up on a map of St. Pete. "Looks like she might be at our old house."

Reese and Kara exchanged glances. Kara had an eyebrow raised again. "You two share locations?"

"We're still each other's emergency contacts. It's for safety."

"It'll be a shady day in Hades before any of my exes get my location," Kara muttered.

"Why, are you guys volunteering to be my emergency contacts?"

"None of our business," Reese said, her palms up.

"It is vaguely stalker vibes." Kara added, "But then again, she's a big girl. Knows how to turn it off. Maybe she wants you to be able to find her."

I pocketed my phone and Murphy trotted to the door.

"No joke though, I'm really invested in this now," Kara said. "Kinda want to know what she says."

Reese shook her head.

I opened the door. "If you see my old house on fire in a few minutes, you'll know why."

"You still want to go shooting later?" Reese asked.

"Yeah. Pick you up this afternoon?"

"Let me know if things go badly with Cassidy, I'll bring the bigger ammo so you can shoot out your anger."

"I'm not angry."

"We'll see."

TWENTY
RELAPSE

MURPHY and I drove the two miles to my old neighborhood in silence. The house Cassidy and I had shared while married was a rental now, mostly short-term vacationers or snow birds. I was between renters at the moment so the house ought to have been empty. But Cassidy knew that too if she'd checked the schedule.

Her rental car was in the driveway of our single story ranch house so I parked in the shade of the oak out front. The lawn was looking dry. I made a note to modify the sprinkler schedule when I had a chance and left Murphy in the Jeep.

It always felt strange to knock at the door of my own house, but I gave the front door a couple of raps with my knuckles before trying the door handle. It was unlocked.

The living room was cozy and well-lit. A comfortable couch sat in a sitting area that blended into an open kitchen and dining room. No one was in evidence, but the Amazon Echo on the counter was playing the local weather forecast.

The bedrooms were in the back, off a hallway that terminated with a door to the back yard. There were vague noises coming from the master bedroom. I made my way down the hall.

"Cass? You here?"

I turned the corner into the bedroom and nearly collided with her coming out.

"Oh geez!" She had her AirPods in and hadn't heard me coming. "Luke. You scared the hell out of me." She pulled the earbuds out of her ears. "What are you doing here?"

"I was about to ask you that."

She glanced at her phone quickly, then put it in the pocket of the gray romper she had on. "Nothing. I was just taking some pictures."

"What for?"

She shifted her stance and rested a hand on her hip. "Well, if you must know, I was thinking about talking to a realtor. See what this place is worth these days."

She swallowed, her eyes roaming my face.

"You want to sell."

"I don't know. Maybe. I was going to see what the market was like before I brought it up. With all that's going on with my family, I was thinking it might be time we talk about doing something different."

I clenched my jaw and bit back the words that wanted to erupt. Keeping it together was always the right play, so I spoke as evenly as I could manage. "Why?"

"You know why."

We were too close. It had been a long time since we'd been in this room together, but it felt familiar. Too familiar. Cassidy with her hair up, the long line of her neck meeting her tan shoulders and the thin spaghetti straps of the lightweight romper. Her brilliant eyes and fresh skin. She smelled like a damned flower. That king bed behind her had once been ours. It brought back more unwelcome memories. A lot of them.

Cassidy shifted her stance and crossed her arms. "You didn't say why you were here."

"Something happened. In the case about Chris."

"Don't tell me they found him?"

"No. Not that kind of news." I rubbed a hand over the back of my neck. This was harder than I thought. But there was nothing else for it. I took a breath. "It has to do with your sister and that vacation we took with her and Chris to Puerto Rico."

Her brow furrowed.

"I never told you. But Ava came on to me one night while we were there. Tried to—I don't know—hook up or something. Nothing happened. But it's come up again. And someone took a video that shows her kissing me. A detective has the video now. Might make a play like it's relevant to the case."

Cassidy took a tighter grip on her elbows but didn't speak.

"You aren't taking this like I expected. I figured you'd be furious."

Cassidy swallowed and looked at the closet. "It's because I already knew."

"Ah."

"I didn't *know*, know. But I heard you come in that night. You smelled like Chanel, so Ava, obviously. You two were super weird with each other the next day. I knew something had happened."

"You never asked."

"You didn't tell me."

"Felt like we had enough worries at the time. You were a new hire at the airline, had a lot of stress. I didn't want to give you any more to carry."

Cassidy exhaled a long breath. "I always knew Ava might try something with you. You aren't the first guy I've dated that she's jumped."

"Sorry to hear that."

"The first boyfriend of mine that she slept with, she claimed she was 'testing' him. Proving he wasn't good enough for me."

"I'm having a hard time thinking of anything shittier than that."

Cassidy nodded but then shook it off. "It's okay. I know you never cheated on me."

"No. I didn't. But how are you so sure?"

"Come on. I *know* you, Luke. I know the kind of man you are and that would have eaten you up inside. It would have changed you. And as someone who has *tried* to change you, I know how hard that is to do." She shook her head.

"Well, thanks. Makes me feel better."

"Besides. You weren't gone long enough that night."

"How do you mean?"

She gave me the look that meant I should be quicker on the uptake. "I've *been* with you, Luke. Your idea of a quickie takes twenty minutes. If you had shagged my sister that night it would have taken you longer."

That got half a smile out of me. "I guess I'll take that as a compliment."

"Yeah. Well, you can have that one for free." She brushed some of her hair behind her ear. "Duration was never your problem."

"I had other problems."

Cassidy bit her lower lip and met my gaze again. "Yeah. You did. Though sometimes I think, maybe I was the one being stupid. And just . . . young. The things that mattered so much then seem like maybe they shouldn't have been such a big deal."

The vulnerability in her eyes was palpable. It seemed to be affecting the air between us.

"I'm probably just feeling nostalgic being back in this house," she added, "thinking about selling it. I'm getting emotional."

I put a hand to her shoulder, ran it down her bare arm. "Makes sense. Lot of good times in this place."

The energy in touching her was electric. The heat of her bare skin under my palm.

She moved into me, my touch a trigger. Her head came to rest just below my chin as she wrapped her arms around my waist. The familiar scent of her shampoo nudged me. A hint of something else familiar on her skin. Sun lotion maybe.

She moved her hands onto my back as we stood there breathing each other in.

I slipped my arms around her too, my fingers running over her shoulder blades and down to the small of her back. She slowly tilted her face up to mine and we stared at each other, hungry for more contact.

My lips were slowly closing the distance to hers. I could count all the freckles on her nose. Her heartbeat was faster with her body pressed against me. Or maybe it was mine that was speeding up.

Her hands slid up my chest, then she rose on her tiptoes and our lips finally met—collided—then crashed, the pressure of her mouth on mine growing firmer with each ravenous kiss.

I inhaled her scent like I'd been drowning without it. How long had I waited to feel *this* again?

My arms clenched around her now, crushing her to me.

It was easy. Familiar. Our bodies melting into each others like we were built for it. I lifted her, one hand scooping her from the floor with an unflinching grip on her ass.

We made it to the bed in three steps and crashed down onto it, a mess of hot breath and wet lips. My skin shivered with the touch of her. I pinned her wrists to the bed above her head and let my mouth wander down her neck to her collar bone.

She let out a slight moan as our hips ground together, but as my hands found their way to the thin shoulder straps of her romper, she whispered, "Wait. Wait, stop."

I stopped.

She panted beneath me, her mouth reddened from the friction of our kisses. "We can't do this. You have a girlfriend already."

Shit.

I lifted my body off hers and slid to one side. I dragged my hands from her burning skin, forcing myself to regain control.

Cassidy covered her eyes with her palms and slid her fingertips into her hair. "Oh God. This is crazy."

"We've had worse ideas."

She focused on the ceiling fan. "I'm probably just ovulating or something."

"That's not an excuse I get to use."

"I saw you with that girl yesterday, and now I can't get it out of my head. I'm being irrational and possessive."

I sat up and faced the wall, glaring at it to keep myself from turning around. "Marie's not my girlfriend. It was one date. It just went farther than I planned. So I don't know what she is yet."

"Okay." Cassidy's voice was soft behind me.

"I'll go."

"I think that's best."

Damn it. What was I doing?

I stood. When I finally turned around, she was still lying there, staring at me.

"I'm sorry," she whispered.

"You don't have anything to apologize for."

"Now you see why we should sell this house?"

I was starting to see her reasoning.

But as I walked through the door, I punched my knuckles to the doorframe. "I'm never selling this house."

TWENTY-ONE
REVELATION

AS FAR AS I was concerned, Saturday afternoons in St. Pete were made for three things: the beach, bikinis, and beers. There was a text on my phone from Marie with a photo showing two of the three. It was her point of view in a lounge chair with her dark legs stretched toward a watery horizon. The text read "Join me?"

On any other Saturday it would have been an easy decision. A quick turn west toward the beach and I could be lounging beachside and popping the top on a can of Modelo in fifteen minutes. As it was, I was still reeling from the unexpected collision with Cassidy. And instead of being with either woman, I was driving into Snell Isle, headed toward the home of a lady I didn't want anything to do with.

My conversation with Cassidy, for all its frustration and confusion to my libido, had given me the confidence to confront Ava. The last thing I needed was the cops all over me as a suspect in Chris's disappearance. If Ava had given them the Puerto Rico video, I had every intention of getting in front of it fast.

Heading toward the bridge to Overlook Drive, I spotted a car coming the opposite direction that couldn't have been anymore noticeable if it was on fire. The matte gold Lamborghini Aventador.

I was far enough away that I might not be recognizable myself yet. Just another dude in a Jeep with a dog. We were an abundant species in this town, but I would be recognizable soon enough.

I slowed, mentally dreading the mere proximity of Johnny Overspray.

He'd better not expect a wave as he went by.

But our passing became an immediate impossibility. The Aventador turned at the bottom of the bridge and pulled into the parking lot of the local Catholic church. It was another ten seconds till I passed the driveway myself. There were a few other cars in the lot. Saturday afternoon mass? I hadn't pegged Johnny as a church-goer.

I continued over the bridge and wound my way through Shore Acres to Venetian Isles. Overlook met Grand Canal and ultimately the cul-de-sac where the Carter home sat. I pulled into the driveway.

Murphy didn't bother with his tour of the yard this time around. He went straight to the front door and let out an excited bark.

"Wait for me, buddy."

I hadn't even made it to the doorbell when the front door opened. Harper threw her arms wide and welcomed the dog into them. "I knew that was a Murphy bark!"

The dog bathed her neck in licks and his tail was a blur.

"You've got good ears," I said.

"Auntie Cass isn't here," Harper said, not bothering to look up from the dog squirming in her arms.

"I know. Just left her at our old house, actually. Your mom around?"

"Nope."

"Ah. You know when she'll be back?"

"Not sure. She went to church."

"Really?"

"Yeah. Said she was going to pray for Dad."

"Huh. You didn't want to go?"

She shrugged. "I used to go a lot. But not anymore. Mom said she wanted to go by herself anyway."

"You stay home by yourself now?"

"Sometimes. I have a phone so I can text. It doesn't do the Internet though, which is lame."

"Maybe it's the Internet that's lame."

"Are you gonna give me a speech about how when you were my age there was no Internet and you only played with wooden toys and walked to school in the snow and stuff?"

"Not now. You must have heard that one."

"That's what dad always tells me. He says I need to be thirteen to get on the Internet and even then he wants to check everything so I don't get catfished by some creepy old man pretending to be a boy."

"Seems reasonable."

"And I said, 'what if I don't even like boys?' And he said 'that's a bridge we can cross if we get to it.'"

Her impression of Chris was pretty good.

"Do you like boys?"

"Maybe. None of the ones at my school though. They're all dumb."

"Fair. Maybe shop around later once you get the Internet."

She nodded and kept petting the dog, and he looked about as happy as he knew how to be.

"You want to keep Murphy for a few hours?"

Her eyes brightened. "Really?"

"Yeah. I was thinking about going up to the gun range later

anyway. Would be nice if I didn't have to leave him at the boat. Give me an excuse to come back by and say hi again later, too."

"Can I feed him?"

"Sure you can. I'll be back by in a few hours, okay?"

"Okay. Oh, wait. I made you something." She dug in her pocket and pulled out a bracelet made of braided leather cords and dark wooden beads. She handed it to me.

"This is fantastic. You're great at this."

"I know."

"Let me know if Murph gives you any trouble, okay?"

"Thanks, Uncle Luke. Come in, Murphy. I've got a stuffed squirrel I can throw for you!"

Murphy never even looked back.

Walking back to my vehicle, I inspected the gift I'd been given. I wasn't an expert on grief or trauma in children, but I was starting to suspect Harper's denial phase was exhibiting itself in bracelet form.

I tied on the bracelet and tightened the knot with my teeth, then fired up the Jeep and reversed course toward downtown. But when I crossed over the bridge, I turned right into the St. Raphael's parking lot. It had filled significantly. Looked like mass must have started. I did a lap around the parking area. There were still plenty of open parking spaces, but no gold Lamborghini. Ava's white Lexus SUV was there though. I parked the Jeep near it and got out.

Like a lot of Florida architecture, the church complex was built in the Spanish style, with terra-cotta tile and faux adobe walls. A plaza divided the church from an elementary school and featured palm trees and a bell tower. I strode into the lobby of the church vaguely self-conscious of my T-shirt and jeans. What was God's dress code these days?

Jesus was a sandals guy. I figured I was okay.

There was a decent crowd inside the church for a sunny

Saturday. Not packed, but a youngish priest and maybe a hundred souls spread out in a half circle of a congregation. The cantor was doing an admirable job belting out a responsorial psalm considering she looked about eleven months pregnant. I slid into a pew in the back and had a look around.

The place was pretty. Lot of natural light and high wooden beams. A crucified Christ loomed large over the altar but he was resurrected in a painting on the lower wall. The church boasted a smattering of stained glass and the requisite complement of pious bowed heads and song books. But it was notably missing one element.

Ava Carter.

She was nowhere in sight.

I lingered five minutes in the pew. That was as long as it took for the congregation to rise to their feet again and obscure my exit. When I walked out to the parking lot, my soul didn't necessarily feel any lighter, but it interested me to know I wasn't the parish's only absent sinner.

REESE and I were putting rounds downrange an hour later. She finished perforating the paper silhouette's torso with a dozen clean shots and turned to me with the pistol's slide open. "So you think Ava was running around on Chris, or what?"

We had a selection of weapons on the table, all empty, but I'd preloaded the magazines at the rear table. I slid one into a Glock and racked the slide. We had the target at ten yards to start. Reese had spent hundreds of hours at the range alongside the snipers she worked with as an intel officer. This distance was nothing for her, but I needed the warm up.

"What good reason would Ava have to ride off with a plane salesman tonight when she no longer has a plane?" I took aim.

"You don't technically know she left with him."

"True. But I know she lied to Harper." I squeezed off the first round and it punctured the target two inches left of where I'd been aiming. I frowned and fired again, this time overcompensating two inches to the right. "If she isn't up to something, why lie?"

"She could be protecting the kid from something unpleasant."

"Garbanza certainly matches that description." My third round went where I wanted it. I put a fourth through the same spot to be sure.

"So she's got a secret reason Overspray wants to see her."

"And the two less-than-secret ones I can think of. In fact he mentioned them to me when I saw him." I put my fifth and sixth rounds through the silhouette's chest, then adjusted the target out to fifteen yards.

"I don't think she intended those to be subtle when she bought them," Reese acknowledged. "But what do you think this has to do with Chris? He found out she was cheating on him and killed himself from grief?"

"Maybe. Or it could be Overspray got rid of his competition."

Reese screwed up her face. "You think Overspray has that in him? Murder?"

"I don't know." My next two rounds went through the number one on the target's paper gut. "I wouldn't have thought so, but people do stupid things out of envy. That detective who grilled me said most crimes boil down to money or sex. I might have just found a motive for the latter."

"Johnny's flashy. Maybe Ava thought he'd give her some security. She's got money trouble, he gets a chance to play the white knight."

"Except he doesn't even get her daughter's name right." I unloaded a barrage of bullets into the silhouette's head, then stopped to check my work. All but one had gone where I wanted.

Room for improvement.

I ejected the magazine, then held the pistol pointed downrange while I ejected the last round from the chamber and caught it with my left hand as it fell.

"You still do that thing where you count your rounds?"

"You can't save the last round for yourself if you don't count."
I balanced the last bullet in my open palm.

"Not sure if you've noticed, but we aren't stuck in a downed
helo behind enemy lines anymore."

"Today we aren't." I handed her the extra round. "You're
welcome to shoot it."

Reese reset the target to the farthest it would go, then put the
round cleanly through the target's head.

"Show off."

She smirked.

We each put a total of a hundred rounds through targets and
walked out of the range smelling like gun smoke.

Reese tucked her pistol case into the back of my Jeep.
"What's next? Confront Ava?"

"Johnny first. I want to see if their stories match."

"Fun. I'll come with."

"I'm sure you and Kara have more fun things to do on a
Saturday night."

"I've still got five bucks on you punching this guy's lights out.
I don't want to miss it."

"Ever think *you* might be the angry one in our friendship?
Maybe you should punch him."

"Oh we both know I would. That's no mystery."

I climbed into the Jeep and got buckled. "All I want out of
this, is for the situation to get resolved, and we get back to life as
usual. I could've been at the beach drinking beers with a
beautiful girl right now, not chasing Ava's misdeeds."

"We know where Overspray lives?"

"Feather Sound somewhere. Realtor girl I know sold him his
condo a couple years ago. Assuming he hasn't moved."

Reese volunteered to go down the Instagram rabbit hole of
my realtor friend's sales postings while I drove. The realtor had

tagged Garbanza in the post and it wasn't long till we had the address from the listing.

Garbanza's condo was expensive but cookie cutter, with several just like it on either side. I parked down the street and we eyed the place from a distance. If the Lambo was there it was in the garage.

I checked my watch. Ava's cover of being at church wouldn't have lasted this long. I doubted she would be here now even if Johnny was back. But my time at the range with Reese would have given him time to return.

"I'll go see if he's there. If not, we can stake the place out a bit."

"Look at us. Doing *Magnum P.I.* shit."

"You know that show?"

"Watched a lot of reruns as a kid. My dad used to love it."

"That's funny. I watched with my grandpa." I slid out of the Wrangler. "I'm the tall one. I call Magnum."

"Hell no. I rock a Hawaiian shirt like it's my job. You fly helicopters, so you're T. C."

"This needs further debate."

We made it to the front walk and up the steps. A giant television glowed through a front window but the lights in the place were dimmed. There was a camera on the doorbell so our visit wasn't going unnoticed. I didn't care. I wasn't the one with the secrets. I rang it.

After thirty seconds of no response, I tried it again. Then I turned to Reese. "No joy."

"We wait?"

"I'm going to take a look around back. That listing showed a pool. Maybe they're catching the sunset from the deck."

"I'll watch the front from the car."

I made my way around the side of the condo. The white plastic gate was cheap and unlocked. My feet crunched coquina shells passing the air conditioning unit and a few poorly watered palms. The lawn out back was microscopic, most of the outdoor real estate given over to a pool with multicolored lights at the bottom. They changed from teal to violet as I watched. The pool was heated. Johnny's electrical bill had to be hefty.

The back yard faced a manmade lake. Nice view. Sun was setting in a fiery show of reds and oranges. No Johnny though.

My phone vibrated in my pocket.

Reese.

I answered.

"What color did you say that Honda was with the dog that attacked Murphy?"

"Baby-shit green. Why?"

"Green Honda just pulled up out front. Couple of guys in it. They're getting out now. Loitering on the front walk."

"Get some video for me."

"Roger that." She disconnected.

This was news. A-hole from the airport showing up at Overspray's place? Now I had two people to set straight.

I mulled my options while I walked back around the side of the condo and peeked over the fence.

The two guys on the front walk looked Latin. One was definitely the guy from the airport. The tigres tattoo wasn't in evidence today. He wore a black synthetic bomber jacket over his black jeans and white tee. His buddy had the same penchant for neck tattoos, but was showing them off with a tank top. Bomber Jacket was smoking a cigarette. After a minute he flicked it on the lawn.

Tank Top walked up the steps and rang the bell. He got the same answer I did.

Bomber Jacket took out his phone and dialed a number.

Sounded like he got voicemail.

"Where you at, cabrón?" This was followed by more swearing.

He jerked his head toward the road and he and his buddy walked back to the car. I couldn't hear anything else they were saying. That wasn't useful. So I opened the gate.

"Hey. Can I help you boys?"

Bomber Jacket turned around. He lowered his phone. "Who are you?"

"Doug's Landscaping."

Tank Top paused at the edge of the lawn to assess me.

Bomber Jacket tucked away the phone and squinted. "I fucking know you. Where I know you from?"

"*Home and Garden* magazine. They did a big spread on us. Had my picture in there and everything. You got a message for John, you need me to tell him anything?"

"I look like I need you in my business?"

Tank Top lumbered closer and encroached on my space. We were only about two yards apart now. He was muscular, but fat too. I had several inches on him but he probably outweighed me by thirty pounds.

"You're that guy from the airport. Dog guy." Bomber Jacket turned toward his buddy. "This guy hit Capitán in the back with a fucking antenna. Big welt. Still swollen."

"Why you gotta hit his dog, man?" Tank Top added some flexing to the question.

"You mean that Cujo reincarnation that tried to murder everything in sight? It's got a boo-boo? How terrible."

"That's animal abuse. Capitán es tranquilo. You ain't got no reason to be hittin' him. Maybe I bust you up with an antenna, see how you like it."

"Maybe you try. See how tranquilo you're feeling after."

That did the trick. Tank Top came at me with a big swing. I pivoted and took it in the shoulder, but I'd used the pivot to wind up, and I unloaded my hips with a right cross, hitting him across the nose at an angle. It hurt my fist too, but as he reeled back, his nose turned into a fountain of blood and surprise.

"Pinche culo," he muttered through the blood. He fumbled at his upper lip as he regained his footing. His fingers came away dark red.

He wasn't out of commission yet, but he was no longer my biggest problem. Bomber Jacket pulled a pistol and aimed it at me.

"You just made a big fucking mistake, pendejo."

"I do that from time to time."

He squinted again. "You smiling while I send you to hell?"

"We'll go together, I guess." I lifted my chin toward the street behind him. He turned slightly and spotted Reese. She had her Kimber 9mm aimed at his back.

"S'up, dickwad," she said.

He cursed under his breath, weighing his choices.

"She won't miss at this range. Trust me," I said.

Tank Top had paused his bleeding all over himself long enough to consider the situation. Looked like he was regretting not carrying something more intimidating than the meat hammers he had for fists.

Bomber Jacket slowly lowered his pistol and tucked it back into his waistband, but kept glaring at me as he did it. Reese didn't lower anything.

"Let's go," he said.

"Puta madre." Tank Top spat some blood that flecked my shoes, then he turned away.

"Remember me if you have any landscaping needs," I replied with a wave. "I have a great special called 'Buy one, go fuck yourself.'"

They climbed back into the Honda while Reese circled around to my position, her pistol still up.

The Honda made a lot of racket as it started, and they burned some rubber into the street, the exhaust sounding like someone murdering a kazoo.

Once the taillights were out of sight, Reese finally put her gun away.

"Took you long enough," I said. "I think a real Magnum would have been quicker."

"Or the true Magnum is the one who remembered their gun."

"Still needs discussion."

We walked back toward the Jeep together. Reese slapped me on the shoulder. "Told you we'd have a fun Saturday night." She put her pistol back in its case. "Maybe I do deserve a raise."

I only took one look back toward the house. For a second I thought I caught one of the upstairs blinds moving. But if it had moved, it was still now.

TWENTY-THREE
FLOAT

CASSIDY OPENED the door at Ava's place when I made it back for my dog. I'd already dropped Reese at home and now my watch read past nine.

My former wife put a finger to her lips as she let me in, and I made my way into the living room where Harper lay asleep on the couch. Murphy was resting on her feet and he yawned when he saw me.

"Tired each other out?"

"She crashed around eight-thirty."

A novel lay open on the end table next to the armchair, a glass of red wine beside it.

"No Ava?"

"Not home yet. She texted me that she ran into some old friends and decided to get dinner out."

"You call her?"

"Should I? I figured she could use the distraction."

Harper let out a whimper in her sleep. Didn't envy whatever bad dreams she was having these days.

"Should I get her to her room?"

"I didn't want to wake her, but if you think you can carry her, that would work."

Murphy climbed off the couch and I scooped up Harper, gently transferring her to my arms. She nestled her cheek on my shoulder, but didn't wake as I stood with her. Cassidy led the way down the hall, opening the bedroom door ahead of us, and I angled Harper through.

After Cassidy turned down the bedsheets and I slipped Harper's feet under them, Harper rolled into her pillow with a satisfied sigh and was back to a gentle snoring shortly after. I followed Cassidy into the hall and she eased the door shut behind us.

"She gets much taller and I'm going to have trouble managing that."

Cassidy nodded. "She'll tower over me one day."

When we reached the living room, she planted her hands on her hips and faced me. "What's going on that has you so concerned?"

"Ava never made it into church tonight, and I don't think her story about meeting friends will hold water." I filled Cassidy in on the details of my visit to St. Raphael's and the subsequent visit to John Garbanza's condo.

"You don't actually know they were together. Could be coincidence."

"Sure. But they know each other. Maybe it's all part of his play for Archangel. I don't know if it has anything to do with Chris, but what are the odds that it's entirely unconnected?"

"So you expect me to jump all over her when she gets home, see what she's been up to with Johnny?"

"I don't expect anything. Just want you to know that Johnny seems like he's tied into something sketchy. Those guys I ran into on his lawn weren't his average clients. I know guys like that and if Ava is hanging out with Johnny, she should be careful. You too. They gave me hardcore ex-con vibes."

"And you pissed them off. That your idea of level-headed decision making?"

"Probably not my sharpest move, but I can take care of myself. I just don't want Ava stepping in some mess of Johnny's if he is seeing her."

"You're sure you're not just looking for things to hate about Johnny after your talk with my dad?"

"There's never been a shortage of things to dislike about Johnny. I just don't want him causing any more damage with your family."

"What makes you think it's connected to Chris?"

"Didn't take a genius to see how obsessed Chris always was with Ava. And why not, she's his wife. But what if he found out she was cheating on him and couldn't take it? People have done crazier things for love."

Cassidy wore a frown.

"You don't buy it?"

"Maybe if it was the first time. But he took her back once already."

"She's cheated before?"

Cassidy walked over and picked up her wine. "You remember that couple, Vera and Mark Russell, they used to hang around with? We did a game night with them once a long time ago. That game you liked with the trains?"

"Vaguely remember that. I remember winning."

"Mark and Ava had a thing. She said it was a one-off mistake. Chris was crushed, but they patched it up. No more game nights with the Russells obviously."

"Shit. Ava's really put him through the wringer. That's not more reason for him to cash it in?"

"And leave Harper? I don't know. I guess it's possible, but if

Ava got away with it once, I kind of think he'd keep taking her back."

"So where does that leave us? Chris was killed? The detectives are looking at homicide."

"By Johnny?"

"Is it impossible? If he wants Ava, Chris has her. Johnny wants Chris out of the way?"

"Ava would never be involved with something like that. If she found out, they'd be done. How could he expect to hide something like that from her?"

"You don't think there's any way Ava could be in on it?"

"*Murder* Chris?"

I put a finger to my lips and she glanced at the hallway and lowered her voice.

"No way. My sister's not anyone's idea of a perfect wife, but she's no killer."

"Fine. Well, whatever happened to Chris, I think you need to have a conversation with Ava about Johnny and see what she says."

"I'll talk with her when she gets home. But you should go. You being here when she gets back won't help my credibility."

"Why, did you tell her about this afternoon?"

"What? Our makeout session? No. That was nothing."

"Didn't feel like nothing."

"Well, it's nothing she needs to know about, and it's nothing that's going to happen again tonight because you're leaving." She put a hand to my bicep and pushed me toward the front door.

I walked onto the porch with Murphy on my heels. Cassidy stopped at the doorpost. I turned to face her. "Be careful. Lock your doors."

"I'm a big girl. I'll be fine."

"These guys I pissed off tonight drove a green Honda in case you see one. Exhaust sounds like a coked-up bumble bee."

"This door is locking and not opening again the second you leave."

"Will you call me when you talk to Ava?"

"You must be loving this. Since I used to think you were the one with the messed up family."

"Still no competition there. Yours has a long way to go."

"Be careful tonight," she said.

"I'm always careful." I leaned back into the doorway and kissed her on the mouth.

As our lips separated, she whispered, "No you're not." She still had her eyes closed. When she finally opened them, she pushed me. "Get out of here."

I walked off the porch and headed for the Jeep. I only took one look back, and by then the door was closed.

That kiss felt good. But I was going to have to stop doing that.

I shifted into gear and took off down the road, but instead of heading south to the marina, I went north. Maybe the altercation with those dudes still had my blood up. Maybe it was Cassidy, but something in me wasn't ready to let things lie for the night.

Discovering those assholes on Johnny's lawn also meant that maybe their hanging around the airport had nothing to do with my brother, and my fears that he might be up to something at Whitted were unfounded.

Cassidy might not have been ready to pin the Carters' current difficulties on Johnny Overspray or a plot to take Chris's place in the family, but the more I replayed the conversations I'd had about Johnny lately, the more the whole thing stunk. He'd even buttered up Dale Dobbs on the attempted Archangel deal. Getting in good with Ava's dad in advance of something bigger? Allaying suspicion? Maybe it was all business for him. Use Ava as an in for the sale, then dump her later. Wouldn't surprise me.

My dislike of Johnny hadn't lessened by the time I reached his condo.

I tucked my Sig into my waistband this time as I crossed the road. The windy Jeep ride had reinvigorated Murphy and he trotted ahead to investigate new turf. I had no Reese covering my back this time, but at least I had some company.

The house looked the same as it had earlier, the TV still glowed from the interior of the living room, but with the sun down, that seemed strange. No one had shut the downstairs blinds for any type of privacy.

I walked up the front steps and made for the doorbell, but Murphy beat me to the door. As was his habit, he nudged the crack of the door with his nose, and to my surprise, the door swung open.

That certainly hadn't been ajar before.

Murphy started in, but I called him back to me. "Hang tight, buddy. Hey, Johnny! You home?"

I took a grip on the doorknob and stepped inside. The front room echoed with the banal banter of two ESPN sportscasters. No real people.

"Johnny!"

My shout brought no response except blowing from the overworked air conditioner as it blustered to bring down the surprising amount of humidity in the room.

Overhead can lights were on in the kitchen, bathing the space in dayglow white. Murphy trotted around, sniffing at the cabinets.

A mosquito buzzed past my ear and I snatched at it with my left hand, grabbing blindly. I opened my palm to find the bug smashed to my knuckles in a bloody smear. Not my blood.

I pulled the Sig from my waistband and moved through the kitchen to the dining room where I found the sliding door to the deck standing open. The humid air off the lake wafted in unobstructed.

Murphy made his way outside and as soon as he reached the edge of the deck, he barked. It was three steps out till the multicolored lights at the bottom of the pool came into view. The lights were turning yellow, but an up-lit cloud of red spread out from the body of John Garbanza floating face down in the pool.

TWENTY-FOUR

FALLOUT

THE UNIFORMS who responded to my 911 call didn't handcuff me. I appreciated that.

I'd pulled the magazine out of my Sig and left it on the kitchen counter with the slide open before the cops arrived, and met them on the front porch with my hands in plain sight. I doubted most murderers they'd encountered practiced that kind of gun safety, so that probably helped my case.

It wasn't lost on me that my gun had been recently fired and I no doubt had gunpowder residue on my hands and clothes from my trip to the range. Not a great look when calling in a body with what I assumed were gunshot wounds in his back. But I waited and cooperated while more and more squad cars showed up, and eventually Detective Blake Rivers arrived. She was in slacks and a light gray button-down blouse tonight, gun and badge on her hip and looking oddly satisfied at seeing me.

"Figured we'd run into each other again sooner rather than later," she said.

"Never one to disappoint."

"You feel like taking a ride downtown?"

"I've got my dog and my Jeep here. Could meet you there later if you like, unless you're arresting me."

She glanced at the street. "We can chat in my car, how about that? Quieter in there."

She invited me to the passenger side of her vehicle. Murphy watched me from the lawn. Unlike standard cruisers, the detective's car lacked the metal grate dividing the front and back seats. Detective Rivers climbed in the driver's side and set a voice recorder in plain sight on the dash.

"I know people who record whole podcasts in their cars these days," she said. "Great sound quality."

"Good for them."

There were about a thousand cops in the vicinity and one lingered conspicuously near the front of the car. Probably had his body camera on to record me. He took a second to pet Murphy though.

"I didn't shoot him. May as well get that on the record early," I said.

"Hardly anyone I interview shoots anybody, seems like. At least till we talk awhile. Sometimes they change their minds."

I told her about my trip to the gun range and gave her Reese's contact info for verification.

"You have a receipt for the ammo or the lane fee?"

"I can get you a bank statement. Never asked for a receipt."

"We'll follow up with the range tomorrow. They record everything. What else do you want to tell me?"

"You should look into some guys who were here earlier. Green Honda. Mexican. One had a gun for sure. It was the same guy from the airport whose dog attacked mine. They rang the doorbell earlier so the camera would have picked them up."

Rivers nodded along. "You know this because?"

"You'll see me in the video too. Coming to the door once, then talking to those guys. Things got testy."

"Not friends of yours."

"I don't think they liked me much, no."

"How do you know they're Mexican?"

I pulled my phone from my pocket and showed her the photo Tyson had improved for me. "This tattoo is derived from a Mayan style. Gang sign for Los Tigres Yucatan."

"Tigres. Thought that was a West Coast gang. San Diego."

"Not these. Still prison-born but a different coast."

She made a note in her phone.

"What's your relationship to the deceased?"

"He sold shitty planes at the airport. And I think he might have been having an affair with Ava Carter."

Detective River's eyebrows rose at that one. "Okay, I'll bite."

I gave her the rundown of my evening looking for Ava.

"You never actually saw them together."

"People keep saying that. Doesn't mean they weren't. There should be phone records if they planned to meet up."

"You never replied about that video I sent you."

"Because it was irrelevant. I didn't hook up with Ava. That video was the extent of our physical contact."

"It's relevant that someone sent it to me."

"I assumed you got it from Ava."

"Wasn't from her number. I asked and she said she didn't know who sent it."

That gave me pause. "Then who sent it to you?"

Rivers shrugged. "Was hoping you might tell me. The number was a dead end. Burner phone maybe. Who else knew about it?"

I had no idea.

"During my interview with Chris Carter's family, Ava mentioned they wanted to sell their plane. Also said they kept it a secret from you because you apparently hated John Garbanza."

"I *disliked* John Garbanza. He was an irritating person."

"Anyone else irritating you lately? Should I have some squad cars sent to their addresses?"

Murphy flopped over onto his side in the grass but didn't take his eyes off me.

"If you aren't planning to arrest me, I'd like to get going. My dog's tired."

"How would you like to voluntarily leave us your gun for ballistics?"

"It's not the murder weapon. Happy to shoot the flowerbed for you if your team needs a bullet to dig out of something."

"I *can* get a warrant for it."

"I'm sure you can. Let me know if you do."

She drummed the steering wheel a couple of times with her thumbs. "That gun falls off the Skyway tonight, it'll look bad for you."

"Are you kidding? This all looks bad for me. I'm still not your guy, though."

Detective Rivers leaned forward and collected her voice recorder with a sigh. "You'll want to stick around the area. No big trips. Good chance I'll have some more questions for you soon."

"Can't wait." I opened the door and climbed out. Murphy made straight for me, tail wagging.

"Let's get out of here, buddy."

A uniformed officer returned my Sig to me. I carried it to the Jeep with the magazine out and a dozen cops looking on.

A couple of Johnny's neighbors even watched me go from their front porches. One of them was recording on their phone.

I called Ava on the way home. It went straight to voicemail.

"Ava. Call me when you get this. It's important."

My expectations were low but it was worth a shot.

The temperature had come down and the wind whipping in the sides of the Jeep left me chilled.

At a stoplight, I called Cassidy.

No answer. Likely asleep if she was still metabolizing red wine the way she used to.

Even Murphy had his muzzle resting against my shoulder as I drove.

He was done.

I checked my mailbox again on the way into the marina. This time I had no mysterious notes.

It occurred to me that if Landon was in Mexico, then someone else must have jammed the slip of paper with his number into my mailbox.

Someone local enough to find me last night.

Guess they weren't delivering tonight.

I checked my phone. Had a voicemail from a reporter at the Times asking about the emergency landing. And there was a text with a picture from Marie. She was at The Canopy—a rooftop bar within walking distance of the marina.

It would be a welcome escape. Strong drinks. Maybe back to the boat after. I could ignore my day and drink it down the drain in the company of a beautiful woman.

But damn it if some nights didn't require solitude.

I rinsed clean in the shower and crashed into my bed face first. Murphy was already snoring in his dog bed upstairs. I lasted only minutes before sleep took me too, and all my dreams were of floating bodies.

TWENTY-FIVE

HANK

SUNDAY DAWNED IN FOG.

The gray morning mist gave the city an eerie quiet. It would be burned off by noon—the sun always wins in Florida. But for now the city was blanketed and damp.

I pulled my hoodie over my head and wiped the condensation off my thinking chair before my morning sit on the bow. Murphy padded down the gangplank and wandered along the dock in search of pilings to pee on.

I waited past seven till calling Cassidy.

She answered with the tone that implied she wasn't through with her coffee yet. "It's early."

"Ava make it home last night?"

"Yeah."

"You talk to her?"

"Not yet. It was late. She said she was with a friend."

"Friend still alive?"

"What does that mean?"

"Johnny Garbanza is dead. I went by there last night and found him in his pool. Shot twice in the back."

"Oh my God."

I told her the story of my night with the police. "I'm sure they'll be by."

"I only met that guy in passing, but it's weird to think he's dead."

"Let me know when Ava is up. I'd like to talk to her."

Cassidy's assurances that Ava was home gave me some peace. Maybe she was nowhere near Johnny's last night. That would be a relief. I'd be happy to be wrong.

I got dressed and wandered out of the marina in search of food.

The Hangar Restaurant had a good breakfast menu and they knew me there. Planes buzzed in and out of runway 7 while diners wolfed down chicken 'n waffles and biscuits with gravy.

The place didn't seat dogs, but I snuck Murphy out to the veranda. My server, Dominique, gave me a smile when she walked up. "Let me guess. The Wheels Up Bowl?"

"You heard, huh?"

"Everybody's heard by now. You feeling okay? Didn't get banged up, did you?"

"I feel great. And I'll stick with the Eggs Benedict."

"Bacon for Murphy?"

"I'd better sample some too."

"You got it."

I'd only had a sip of my coffee when I felt a weight on my shoulder. I looked up to find the wrinkled brown face of Hank Martin peering down at me. "What is this I hear about my grandson getting a shotgun pointed at him during a flying lesson." His grip on my shoulder was a vice.

"Don't spill the man's coffee, dear." Madeline Coleman-Martin stood beside her husband with a chiding expression on her face. "I'm sure there's an explanation that he's going to give us in *explicit* detail."

I rose from my chair and offered Madeline the seat across from me. "Good morning, Maddie." I leaned over and gave her a kiss on the cheek and a deferential nod.

People stood straighter around Maddie Coleman-Martin. She had that effect. Maybe it was the history. She was a direct relation of Bess Coleman, the first black woman to ever earn her pilot's license, and while she didn't fly much herself, the Martins were significant donors to Sisters of the Skies, the non-profit working to inspire black women to become airline pilots. The name Martin meant something around here and she was a big part of why.

Hank pulled out the seat next to me. He was getting thinner, but at eighty-five still had a presence about him that commanded respect.

"Tyson did have a shotgun pointed in his general direction. From a distance. But he wasn't in danger."

"You understand why we're concerned," Maddie said as she situated a napkin in her lap.

"And pissed off," Hank added.

"Yes, sir. Noted."

Hank finally sat, easing himself into the chair beside me.

"I took Tyson off-field to get him some tailwheel time on a dirt strip. He did great."

"My grandson told me who you visited. Don't think I don't know the history there. I knew your daddy before you did. Tyson may not think it was a significant visit, but he's naive, and I'd like to keep it that way."

"I stopped in to have a word with Earl and Margery. Just as a precaution."

"Because?" Hank pressed.

I waited while Dominique brought more waters for the table and cleared out again.

"I had a call from Landon. Made me wonder what he's up to and if it might affect Whitted."

Hank snorted. "That brother of yours is about as welcome as your father. And Frank can kick rocks."

"I told Landon that whatever he's up to, I'm keeping out of it."

"He's still your family," Maddie interjected. "He's bound to keep turning up."

"He's involved in something down in Mexico from what I can gather. I think he might have found *Tropic Angel*."

"Frank's Mallard?" Hank sat back in his chair and scrutinized me. "Thought that was a total loss."

"According to the FAA's registry it is. But it sounds like Landon might have other plans. He called it a 'jungle resurrection.'"

"Big seaplane like that, hard-to-find parts. Probably cost a fortune to restore. Where's Landon getting the money?"

"Said he owes someone. Knowing him, it's someone we don't want to be anywhere near."

Dominique came back with coffees for the Martins and took their orders. When she was gone again, Maddie spoke. "We heard about your emergency landing in the Seneca. Glad you're okay."

"Press been after you yet?" Hank inquired.

"I've ignored a few calls."

"Good. Last thing we need is more people stirring up the press about the airport. Even a perfect landing like yours, they'll find a way to make it a safety issue and use it to attack us."

"Sharks will be sharks."

"They ignore fifteen thousand car accidents a year in this city, to focus on one incident at the airport. They'll say it's a reason it should all be bulldozed for condos. One slip-up. That's all they're waiting for to come at us again. Like they can't tell they depend on this place day in and day out in ways they never thought of."

"The airport's been here a hundred years, Hank," Maddie said. "We'll make sure it's here for a hundred more." She rested a hand on his from across the table.

"I get a bit fired up on the subject, if you can't tell," Hank said.

"No one better to do it."

He took a breath and looked toward the water. "How's my boat?"

"Still floating. We going sailing soon?"

"We should," Hank nodded. "We should. Teach Tyson a thing or two about how to handle it. I want that boy to know his way around the bay from the water too, not just the air."

"I promise I'l keep him away from shotguns this week. I'm sorry you had cause to worry."

Hank rested a hand on my shoulder. "I always know you'll do the right thing, Luke. Much as I spout off about your daddy and what a troublemaker he was, I know what it took to break away from that. You have more to you than he ever did, and Maddie and me never would have put so much faith in you if we didn't know it."

"You might be the only ones."

"Doubtful. Your reputation on the field suggests otherwise."

"Says the man whose shadow I stand in."

"I'm an old man, Luke. The future of the airport's resting in the hands of younger people like you. Like your friend Reese. Tyson too, as much as he needs a good kick in the pants some days to see it."

"We don't take the responsibility lightly."

"You'd best not," Maddie added.

Our food came and we lapsed into lighter topics. Maddie's non-profit was doing more scholarships. Hank talked baseball. I paid the bill with Dominique behind their backs and got scolded for my efforts by Maddie, but Hank looked appreciative.

We parted ways a half hour later.

Hank waved as they made their way down the sidewalk toward the heart of downtown. Maddie held his hand. Neither of them noticed the unmarked police car parked at the curb or the officer lingering near the bike racks keeping an eye on me.

I checked my phone and noted a missed call from Landon.

If the Martins thought the reputation of the airport was in safe hands with me, they were being set up for disappointment.

COPS FOLLOWED me on my walk away from the airport. Maybe these two never learned to be subtle. Maybe they just didn't care.

I hadn't murdered anyone, so them keeping an eye on me shouldn't have been much of a bother. It did bother me though. No one likes a snoop.

Landon had left a voicemail.

"Hey, Bogey. Call me back. It's important."

He read off the number.

That was it.

Bogey had been my dad's joke since I was a toddler. "Watch out, Landon! You've got a bogey on your six." He'd come swooping in and scoop me up in his arms. "Got him!"

I'd laugh, and the moment he set me down, I'd waddle around behind Landon some more.

It had landed me the name 'Bogey' for years. The good years anyway.

Till I got tired of following.

Based on the surveillance I was getting this morning, there

was a strong chance my phone was being monitored by the snoops.

But it was an easy enough problem to solve.

I meandered through downtown, found the coffee shop on Central I frequented on weekends like this. A dozen regulars lounged around chitchatting. I got a few fist bumps. Murphy got cooed at and petted.

Nikki was a brunette with a great tan. Probably going to regret it in a few years, but she'd come from the frigid north of Michigan and now worshiped the sun all year. She had as many bad habits as she did tattoos but she had the natural beauty to get away with both. We'd been out for drinks on occasion so she let me borrow her phone without asking why.

Landon picked up on the second ring.

"What do you want?" I demanded.

"Well, hello, uh . . . Nicole? Thanks for calling."

"Borrowed the phone, so keep it short. I don't want to be rude. Is this call international?"

"Routes through a web address. Nicole won't go broke."

"Let me guess, you still need something."

"Actually, this time I'm doing you a favor. Remember that guy I told you about we had in your area? He wasn't working out and now he's off the job."

"I'm not filling in."

"Turns out he misplaced some funding. A lot of it. Now some people seem to think you might have it. It's putting a target on your back."

"The hell are you talking about?"

"I tried telling them there's no way you're the guy that took it. But they're gonna need some convincing, and I'm worried things might get unfriendly."

The puzzle pieces were starting to fall into place. Johnny

Overspray standing on the hangar ramp showing me a picture of cash on his table. The Mexican guys on his lawn with a gun.

I took a tighter grip on the phone as I hissed into it. "Are you telling me Johnny Garbanza was working for you?"

"Not anymore."

"No shit, Landon. He's dead."

"This is me giving you time to get out of town."

"Johnny was trying to buy Archangel Aviation out from under me. That was *you*?"

"The deal would have been mutually beneficial. Would have brought in a ton of cash to your operation."

"No. You wanted a front. For whatever bullshit you're into, like always." I got up and moved away from the coffee shop, since people were starting to stare.

"Some people I'm dealing with need a legit way to get their hands on some planes. They're giving me the Mallard and setting us up. Figured you'd want in."

"As drug smugglers?"

"A legitimate import/export business. The laws are changing. We'd be set up at a key point in the product chain."

"If I could climb through this phone, I'd strangle you. Those guys in the Honda. Tigres tattoos. They're your people."

"La Reina Tigre's people. It's her land. Her operation. I'm just a facilitator."

"You're a blood-sucking leech. You're a goddamn boil on my ass. I can't believe you'd set me up like this."

"I take it you don't have the cash."

I resisted hurling the phone into the street. Just barely.

"So you need to find who does," he continued. "It would be best for your health if you figure that out soon."

"You're garbage, Landon. You know that?"

"I'm on your side in this."

"The hell you are."

I hung up.

When I walked back to Nikki, she accepted her phone gingerly. "Sounds like your day just took a shit."

"I'd say 'it could be worse,' but I'm not sure that's true."

Damn you, Landon.

Two guys in a car across the street were watching me. I'd been confident they were the cops before. But was I still sure?

I leashed Murphy and walked, keeping an eye out behind me.

I called Ava. Got voicemail.

I tried Cassidy next and she answered.

"Ava says she was out with friends last night. Drinks at The Canopy and the Vinoy. Says that's it and to leave her alone. Sticking to her story."

"You believe her?"

Her silence was too long.

"Put her on the phone."

"She says she doesn't want to talk to you."

"Tell her that she talks to me or I come over there and bang on the door till she does."

"I doubt that's going to solve anything."

"Tell her that Johnny was mixed up with some dangerous people and now those people are pissed off. If she knows *anything* about it, I need her to tell me."

"Hang on."

I glared at more traffic and pedestrians while I waited what felt like an eternity. She finally came back on. "She says she'll come to see you tonight. Wants to meet you at your boat."

"Why not now?"

"Says she's busy."

"Cass. Some serious shit is going down and I need answers."

"Okay. I'll make sure she shows up."

"Be careful."

I cut through several parking lots and alleys. If I still had a tail at the moment, I couldn't spot them. I wasn't sure if I felt better or worse about that.

I now had one more call to make.

Marie practically purred as she answered the phone. "Well, I didn't expect you to be one of those 'wait three days before calling a girl' type guys, but I'm hoping you're worth the wait."

"It's been an unusual few days."

"Tell me you're taking me out tonight and I'll forgive you."

"Sadly, I've got plans. But I'm hoping I might ask a favor. You were at The Canopy last night?"

"So you did get my texts. Thought maybe you forgot to pay your phone bill."

"If I send you a photo of a woman, could you tell me if you saw her there? Supposedly she was there for several hours."

"You don't reply for three days, then need me to play detective about another woman?"

"She's not a romantic interest. It's a piece of a puzzle I'm trying to put together."

"What kind of puzzle?"

"A sucky personal kind."

"Ah."

"I can explain the situation if you want me to. Doesn't reflect many of my best qualities, though."

"You don't owe me anything."

"Maybe I should. Can I send the picture?"

"This have anything to do with your ex-wife?"

"Some. Her being back has complicated things. I'll admit that."

"Thought that might be the problem. Is she part of your plans tonight?"

"Only tangentially."

"I'm not a second-place kind of girl, Luke."

"No. You're not. And if our date had happened anytime in

the last year other than this weekend, we'd be having a different kind of day right now. You'd have trouble getting rid of me."

"So . . . poor timing?"

"The worst."

Her long silence on the phone spoke volumes, but when she finally came on again, her voice was even. "Send me the photo."

I pulled a link from one of Ava's social media accounts and texted it.

It only took Marie a few moments of looking.

"No. Didn't see her there. I would've noticed. Who is she?"

"My ex-sister-in-law. She's in some trouble."

"You in trouble too?"

"Maybe. It's getting contagious."

"You're giving me more reasons to steer clear."

"I think it's the best decision right now."

"I'd delete your number, but it sounds like maybe I shouldn't."

"Why's that?"

"You might call me when you need a good lawyer."

TWENTY-SEVEN
WAITING GAME

THERE'S no good reason to be at work on a beautiful Sunday afternoon in St. Pete, but that's where I was. The fog had burned off as predicted and sunshine lit the hangar and glinted off the polished wrench set on top of my tool box.

The work could have waited for Monday, but my hands needed the activity. I had a cylinder off the engine of a customer's Globe Swift and was wrapping up the reinstallation. It was simple work. Focused, and deliberate. The kind of work that drove other thoughts from my brain. Alone in the quiet, I was able to convince myself life was still normal. If I didn't count the car out on the street with a cop in it.

I had the antique plane running again around the time the sun was heading for the horizon. I cowled it up and taxied out to runway seven. One of the best parts of repairing customers planes was all the aircraft I got to test fly. I'd see how well the surveillance team could follow now.

Low clouds speckled the horizon. I took the water route first, south over the Sunshine Skyway Bridge, then north along the white sand beaches. The polished aluminum Swift's wings reflected cloud colors. Oil temps all looked good. The engine purred along like no time at all had passed since the late 1940s when the plane had been built.

I cruised the coastline, low enough to wave the wings at the tourists and local sun-setters.

The sun disappeared into the Gulf as I turned east again.

The city's street lights illuminated beneath me and the runway shone as a beacon ahead. The tower cleared me to land and I greased the plane in on the runway numbers with a chirp of the tires. I said goodnight to the tower controller and rolled back to the ramp relishing the hum of the engine. All was right with the world for at least that one flight.

I closed my hangar and walked home by way of a sandwich at the pub.

Ava's SUV pulled into the marina parking lot the same time I was arriving.

Cassidy was with her.

I held the gate for them while I watched the parking lot and my dutiful tail from the St. Pete Police Department arrived on cue, circling to park in a far-off space across the lot. A few seconds later, another car pulled in and did the same maneuver, brake lights flashing when it found one of its compatriots already on the job. Ava's tail.

Cassidy spotted them too.

"They here for you?"

"I'm popular."

Ava had her sunglasses on for some reason, despite the dark. She strode ahead wordlessly to the *Midlife Crisis* and away from the prying eyes of the cops. I let the women into the boat's living area and flipped on the lights. Murphy took up residence on his dog bed to supervise.

"I appreciate you coming, Ava."

Ava surveyed the boat skeptically, then slumped onto the

couch with her arms crossed. "Cassidy says you have your panties in a bunch about something and I *had* to come talk, so congratulations. I'm here." She checked the time on her phone. "What do you want to talk about?"

"Your open and enthusiastic communication style really shows."

Ava flipped me the middle finger. "How's this for open communication."

Cassidy sighed. "Ava."

"It's fine," I said. "If I was in her shoes, I wouldn't be thrilled at having to talk either, but we either get this out in the open now or pretty soon the cops will be sorting it for us. That or someone worse."

Ava checked her phone again and set it back down. "You have something to drink on this yacht? This seems like the kind of mansplaining that I'll need alcohol for."

I opened the fridge and found a hard seltzer. I poured it over ice for her and set it on the coffee table. "There you go. What were you doing with Johnny Garbanza last night?"

She picked up the drink and sipped it. With her sunglasses still on, it was difficult to discern her expression. "Why don't you tell me what you think is going on and I'll tell you all the reasons you're wrong."

"Johnny is dead, Ava. I found him floating with two bullet holes in his back that didn't come from someone being coy and evasive like you. Cassidy is convinced you couldn't have anything to do with a murder. She doesn't think you have that in you, and I'd tend to agree, but I also know you aren't coming clean with whatever you're up to, and it's time you do before someone else gets killed."

"I've told you. I was out last night with friends. I don't know anything about it."

"You were at The Canopy."

She nodded.

"Only I know you weren't. Because I was, and you were nowhere in sight."

She regarded me cooly. "It's a busy place. You must not have noticed."

"Did you see me?"

She tilted her chin up. "Actually, I did see you. I just wanted to avoid you."

"Right." I put my hands on my hips. "These people—the guys I ran into at Johnny's place last night. They're bad news. Possibly working for a drug lord in Mexico. Word is Johnny screwed them over somehow. He wasn't just a sleazy plane salesman with a ridiculous car. He was connected with the cartel and now they're pissed off. Looking for money Johnny supposedly lost."

"That clearly has nothing to do with me."

"Then why is the ice in your glass shaking?"

She looked down to her trembling hand, then quickly set the glass on the coffee table. "I don't need to sit here and be interrogated." She checked her phone again.

"You have somewhere to be? Something we're keeping you from?"

"Luke." Cassidy was giving me the look that said I was too worked up. Married or not, it was easy to translate.

I caught the nearby puttering of a boat motor outside—someone entering the marina at idle speed.

I took a breath. "Let's try this again." I sat on the couch at the opposite corner from Ava and faced her. "Getting involved with a guy like Johnny isn't a crime. He was flashy and arrogant and I thought he was a prick, but that's only my opinion. If you two were something significant to each other, that's none of my damned business. I just need to know there's nothing from his messy dealings that could leak over into your family."

"Pretty rich coming from the guy with the jailbird for a dad."

"This isn't me casting the first stone. God knows my family is a mess. That's why I'm talking to you. If you had an affair, that's not illegal. It would suck, especially if it was a factor in Chris leaving, but people have affairs. But we do need to inform whoever it is that shot Johnny that you weren't involved in any of his dealings. If we can somehow—"

I stopped talking because Murphy let out a low growl. He sat up and stared at the sliding glass door.

The door flew open and a man in a ski mask leveled a gun at me.

"Nobody move or I blow you to pieces."

TWENTY-EIGHT
RUSE

"EVERYBODY STAY CALM, and nobody gets hurt."

The guy in the ski mask was deepening his voice, adding a layer of intimidation to it. Not an especially muscular guy. No way it was Tank Top from Johnny's lawn yesterday. Plus he didn't sound Hispanic. This guy wore a long-sleeve black T-shirt and dark jeans, gloves on both hands, and had a small satchel slung over one shoulder. The gun was a snub-nose .38.

He kept the gun pointed at me but he addressed Ava. "You. Get over here. You're coming with me."

Ava gave him a long stare. "Why should I?"

"You get your ass over here now or one of these other two gets a bullet." He waved the gun toward Cassidy.

"Hey," I took a step forward. He swung the gun back toward me.

"Let's you and me talk, huh?"

His gun hand was shaking. Adrenaline must be getting to him.

I'd had guns pointed at me by worse—in the last twenty-four hours at that—but nervous people could be dangerous. Whoever this guy was, he didn't do this professionally. If his gun went off I'd rather have it pointed my way than Cassidy's.

"You get here by boat?" I asked. "Heard your motor out there. That a Mercury or a Yamaha?"

"Yama—doesn't matter. You shut up." He yelled at Ava again. "Get over here."

Ava rose and took a few steps toward him. Like a martyr.

"Turn around." The guy produced a couple of zip ties from the satchel. They weren't preset as loops. I was curious how he was going to use them on her and still hold the gun.

There were already a lot of things not adding up about this situation.

"Escape by boat seems dodgy. You think this all the way through, man?"

He waved the gun around some more. "You shut it. Keep your lip zipped and I won't have to hurt anybody. This will all be over in just a minute." Sounded like he was reassuring himself as much as us.

He hadn't distorted his voice as much that time.

Murphy had stopped growling.

Ava had enough years of Krav Maga under her belt that her taking this guy down solo wasn't out of the realm of possibility. I was farthest from him so I looked around at things to throw. My Jeep keys on the counter might be a start. I regretted leaving my gun downstairs. I'd need a distraction for long enough to get me across the room. Once I got this guy's gun away from him, I'd make him eat it.

The guy handed the loose zip ties to Ava. "Use these. Tie your wrists."

I expected Ava to hurl them back in his face, but she took them. She gave me one sideways glance and then set to work making a loop. So much for Krav Maga.

Murphy got off his dog bed and walked across the room to sniff the guy's shoes.

"Hey. Get." He made a vague shooing motion with his foot and looked to me. "Call your dog."

Murphy laid down at the guy's feet and let his tongue hang out.

That's when I decided to open the fridge and get a beer.

"Whoa, hey. What do you think you're doing?" He was probably pointing the gun at me again. I didn't care.

I pulled a pair of Dos Equis from the fridge and brought them back to the counter. There was a bottle opener built into the cabinet so I used that and popped both tops before carrying one over to where Cassidy was sitting. I handed it to her. "Sorry, I'm out of limes."

Her eyes were wide and questioning.

"The entertainment tonight is pretty terrible, huh? If we're going to have to watch it, I think we need beverages." I sank onto the couch next to her and put one arm around her, then put my feet up on the coffee table.

Ava had stopped moving, though she'd managed to get one zip tie around her wrist. The guy in the mask was frozen. They shared a look.

I took a sip of my beer, then sighed. "It's clear there's only one decent actor in this production. May as well take off the mask, Chris. You look ridiculous."

He deliberated a long moment, then lowered the gun. "Shit." He reached up and pulled the ski mask off. His face was sweaty and his hair matted. But for a supposedly dead guy, he was looking pretty good. "How could you tell?"

"Blame it on the dog if it makes you feel better."

"Chris?" Cassidy let her mouth hang open.

Chris turned to Ava. "I told you this was a bad idea."

Ava put a manicured hand to her forehead.

Cassidy shot to her feet. "This was *your* idea? Are you kidding me! Somebody could've gotten killed."

"With that thing?" Ava gestured to the pistol. "Chris wasn't actually going to *shoot* anybody."

"Armed kidnapping, huh?" I asked. "I have to hear how this made sense to either one of you as a Sunday night activity."

Chris turned to Ava again. So did we.

"What?" she asked. "I'm as surprised as you are that he's here."

I laughed.

Maybe it was the accumulated tension of the last few days. The stress of worrying about Chris, the questioning of things with Cassidy. It had built up and all I could manage now was to laugh. My in-laws were being first-rate idiots, but they were alive. Harper's dad was safe. Acting like an imbecile, but a living imbecile.

Then my mind drifted back to Johnny in the pool—the bullet wounds and the blood. My smile faded. I set my beer on the coffee table.

"Tell me about Johnny, Chris. What did you two do?"

"We didn't kill him," Chris blurted out. "I swear."

No part of me had assumed Chris capable of murdering Johnny so that didn't come as a surprise. "Ava?"

She was shaking her head. "This can all still be salvaged if we work it out."

"We've got two cars full of cops in the parking lot," I said. "You don't see me calling them yet, but you'd best get to explaining."

"The truth, Ava," Cassidy added. Her tone was barely controlled rage.

Ava put up her hands. "It's not that big of a deal. We were just going to do a *little* life insurance claim. At first."

"Chris's fake suicide as a money grab," I said.

"Unbelievable," Cassidy muttered.

"You're not the one with collections agencies calling every other day," Ava retorted. "They started coming to the *house*. The house!"

The nerve of them.

"I have to admit you had me going with that snow job at your place the other day," I said. "All that talk about Chris looking up to me and being intimidated to have me help him sell the plane. I fell for that nonsense like an idiot. But there was blood on the hangar floor, too. Where did that come from?"

Chris and Ava shared another glance. Chris looked sheepish.

"We were going to make it look like a possible murder to confuse the cops. Ava read that cases with layers like that are more convincing. But then I had second thoughts and cleaned it up."

"They still found it. Probably made it look even more like a murder."

"I realized that after."

"Told you you should have just left it alone," Ava said.

"Why plan a fake suicide, then switch to murder later?" I asked.

"Because I met Johnny when he wanted to get Dad to sell his part of the airport business," she added, "And I got another idea."

Chris spoke up. "It wasn't personal, Luke. Going after Archangel."

"I have cops investigating me for murdering you. Of course it's personal. Are you the one that sent the video of me and Ava in Puerto Rico to the police?"

Chris swallowed hard but didn't answer.

"You know what? It doesn't matter. If I was trying to cast suspicion on a fall guy, I'd go with a dude from a family full of felons too. But we've got bigger issues. What exactly did you mean when you said you got another idea, Ava?"

Her face contorted like I was asking her to lay an egg. But she finally spoke. "Johnny was going to pay cash for your business if he got it. Like actual cash."

"Oh geez. Don't tell me you went after the money," I said.

"It was five *million* dollars!" Ava said. As if that was an explanation. "And he showed it to me in his house. Just sitting there."

Chris looked nauseated and shaky, his peak of adrenaline replaced by a dose of reality. Ava carried on.

"Johnny thought Chris was dead, and I'd given him the impression that *maybe* I was interested in him," she continued. "So he let me come over a few times."

"You slept with Johnny to steal his money?" Cassidy's voice had reached an intensity I was happy to not be on the receiving end of. She turned on Chris. "And *you* let her?"

"It was a means to an end!" Ava shouted. "An end where *Chris* and I are on a beach drinking mai tais. Not living paycheck to goddamn paycheck with people coming after everything we've got. We were going to disappear."

"Just leave?" Cassidy was red in the face now. "And what? Abandon your family?"

"You would've been *fine*," Ava spat back. "Everyone knows you're Dad's favorite anyway."

I got off the couch.

"Ava. I need you to be clear with me. Did you take that cash from Johnny's last night?"

She ended the staring contest she was having with her sister and gave me an exasperated sigh. "He kept his stupid safe password in his phone. It was so easy to just look at it. It's his own fault!"

I grasped both her shoulders and squeezed. "Ava. Do you have *any* idea who that cash belonged to? You think that money was his?"

"I took it, okay? We took it."

Good Lord.

This was bad.

"That money belongs to a woman named La Reina Tigre. She's head of one of the most dangerous gangs in Mexico. And they've got people in St. Pete right now." I turned to Cassidy. "Where's Harper?"

Cassidy's eyes widened. "She's home by herself."

"Call her," I said. "Right now."

"She's at the house," Ava said. "She's fine. There's cops outside all the time now."

"The cops are following you, Ava. Not Harper. So those cops are here."

Cassidy had her phone to her ear. "She's not answering. Dammit." She hung up and tried again.

"Wait, what's the problem with Harper?" Chris sputtered.

"Keep calling," I said. I snatched my keys off the counter and dropped down the stairs to my berth. My gun was in a clip holster on the end table and I snatched it. I had a pump action shotgun in the closet. I collected that and a box of shells as well.

"What are you doing?" Chris asked from upstairs. "You think Harper is in danger?"

I climbed back up the steps and laid the shotgun on the counter. Then I checked the magazine on my Sig Sauer. "You two numb nuts just stole five million dollars from a Mexican drug cartel. Of course she's in danger. All of us are."

"Oh God." Chris went pale.

"What was your plan tonight?" I asked while I clipped the holster to my belt. "After this ludicrous fake kidnapping? You steal Ava away and then what? Was Harper in on this escape plan?"

"Not yet," Chris said. "Ava had her stuff packed for a trip. But she didn't know where. She thought she was going to her grandparents for a while. We were going to pick her up at the boat slip behind the house tonight and get to the plane. I hid it down at Thompson Airstrip."

"Leaving the country?"

"Bahamas and south. We always wanted to get away to the Caribbean. I have a friend from college who made us new passports. It wasn't as hard as I thought."

"Most dumbass plans aren't hard in the beginning, Chris. It's pulling them off that's difficult."

"Luke, we didn't know it was drug money. I swear. We just thought it was Johnny's. The guy drives a gold Lamborghini for God's sake."

Cassidy shook her head. "Still not answering."

"I'm headed over there." I loaded the shotgun for Cassidy, then handed it to her. "Anyone other than us comes knocking, don't be shy with this. "I turned to Chris. "By the way, you tell someone you're going to blow them to pieces, you want that in your hand." I pointed to the shotgun. "Nobody is losing a limb to that snub nose of yours."

Chris looked down at his gun. "I don't exactly have a lot of experience with stick ups."

"You coming with me?" I asked.

"Yeah."

Murphy rushed to the door too. "Uh-huh. Stay here, buddy. You're sitting this one out."

"Should we call the cops?" Cassidy asked.

"Hang on. Stop!" Ava shouted. "We can still *fix* this. Harper is probably just watching TV and has her phone in another room. We don't want the cops knowing about Chris yet, do we? If he goes out there, we're admitting we lied."

"You stole five million dollars, Ava," I said.

"From *drug* people. They aren't exactly going to be calling the cops about that are they?"

"You still want to try to leave?" Chris asked.

"Why not?" Ava gestured to me. "Unless *he* sells us out, no one else knows we have it."

"I know," Cassidy said.

"You don't want your sister going to jail, do you? I'll even split some of the money with you. Mom and Dad too. They don't need to know where it came from."

I gripped the door handle. "You have worse things to fear than jail right now, Ava. Come on, Chris."

Ava glared at him and shook her head. "Don't."

"It's Harper, Babe. We at least have to check that she's safe. But we don't have to call the cops yet, right?" He turned to me.

I sighed. "They'll be following us anyway. But we go, now."

Ava came to him and clenched his arm. "You're giving up on our plan? After all we just went through? After what I had to do?"

"Don't pretend *that* was the hardship." Chris jerked his arm away. He tucked the .38 into his pants and walked out the door.

Ava looked like she might want to murder him for real this time. Possibly me too.

But Chris walked down the gangplank anyway.

For what it was worth, I was proud of him for that.

I just hoped it wasn't too little, too late.

TWENTY-NINE
STRUCK

"WE SHOULD TAKE THE BOAT," Chris said. "I timed the trip and it's faster."

Venetian Isles was on the water and if we kept up a decent speed, I could see the logic. Must have been part of their getaway plan. Plus we were still out of view from the cops in the parking lot. Taking the boat would keep it that way.

"Okay, let's go."

Chris's twenty-two foot center-console bay boat was tied off along the dock behind the *Midlife Crisis* and it was an easy transfer. I untied the bow line and pushed us away from the dock. Chris made short work of getting out of the marina and into the calm water of the bay. He focused on the dim horizon and pushed the 150 horsepower Yamaha motor wide open. For all his idiocy of the last few days, I was happy to see he still had his priorities straight when it came to Harper's safety.

Once we leveled out on plane, he shouted over the noise.

"You really think someone might try to hurt her?"

The lights of the marina faded behind us as I mulled our options. "I think the faster we act, the safer she'll stay."

We shot across the open water past the St. Pete Pier and up the western shoreline of Tampa Bay. There were a few other boats out, but they gave us a wide berth.

"I'm sorry I got you mixed up in this, Luke. It all got so far out of hand."

"If things were that bad for you, why not talk to somebody? Ava's parents?"

"I couldn't have Ava be the kid that drained their retirement. It was our mistakes, our mess. And I doubt they had enough anyway."

"So sell the house. Sell the plane. That won't get you solvent?"

"We're so far under water on the house we won't make anything. Bank's coming for all of it. It wasn't even worth selling."

"So you were going to run away from your problems."

"Sitting on a beach in another country sounded a lot sexier than bankruptcy."

We hit a residual wake from another boat and salt water sprayed up from the bow and misted us.

"Going on the run. Family thinking you're all dead or kidnapped? Might work for someone like me whose family was garbage, but what kind of life is that for you?"

"We were going to fill them in once we made our escape."

"You're not twelve, man. Running away to foreign countries only works in the movies."

"Maybe. God, I don't know what we'll do now. You think the cops will buy me being gone for some other reason? Maybe we say I just ran out on Ava. That's not a crime."

"You told a lot of lies, Chris, and I don't know how many times I have to tell you this. As long as you have that money, you're in far worse danger than jail."

"But they don't *know* we have it, right?"

"If I figured out that Ava was meeting with Johnny, then someone else could have seen her with him."

What I didn't know was if my involvement had been part of the problem too. Could La Reina Tigre's people have seen me at Ava's? Would they make that connection? If they thought I was the one who had their money, I could have inadvertently put the whole family at risk.

It was on my mind all the way to the house.

The inlet was quiet as we pulled up. I would have preferred to see activity, more boats out or even a barking dog. But it was dead silent. We tied off at the dock and made our way through the back lot.

Lights were out in the house except for something far interior —the kitchen.

The back door was still locked. Chris fumbled with his keys and got the door open. One step though the door, he shouted. "Harp! Where are you, sweetie. Daddy's home!"

The shout faded into silence.

"Harp?" He tried again, checking the den, then the living room. I jogged down the hall to her room and pushed open the door. An iPad lay on the floor. Some show on Netflix was still playing on it. Harper's phone was on the floor too. It was a flip phone lying open on its face. I picked it up and tapped the home button to wake it. It was on the call screen and had two numbers entered. A 9 and a 1.

"Shit," I muttered.

"Luke! Someone's been in the side door to the kitchen."

I walked out to the family room with Harper's phone in my hand.

Chris stared at the phone and then ran past me to her room. He checked the hall bathroom and the master bedroom next, shouting his daughter's name the entire time.

The kitchen's sliding door had been forced open, a pry bar wedged in and the lock dislodged.

My skin prickled.

How long had they had her?

Maybe they hadn't gotten far.

I pulled my phone from my pocket and started to locate the contact for Detective Rivers. But before I could call, a phone rang in my hand.

Only it wasn't my phone. It was Harper's.

The number wasn't listed. I answered.

"Who is this?"

"Oh, I think you know who, Jardinero."

It was loud in the background. A vehicle.

"I never got your name."

"You can call me El Halcón. And it's a name you should remember because I'm going to wreck your world."

"Do you have my niece, Halcón?"

"This little girl makes a lot of noise. So much we had to tape her mouth shut. But she won't be noisy long. You don't come through with what I need, I'm going to feed her piece-by-piece to my dogs."

I closed my eyes, focused on my next breath. "You'll get what you need. Let's make it fast."

Chris came back into the room, eyes wide. "I looked everywhere in the house—"

I held up a finger.

"Is that her? Does someone have her?"

"Sounds like you got company," El Halcón said. "Better not be the cops."

"No cops."

"Let me talk to those bastards." Chris came at the phone, but I held him off with a hand to his chest.

"Tell me where to meet you, Halcón. I'll bring you the cash. We'll get this done."

"You bring the cash. Every cent. But you gotta pay the interest now, holmes. You come in that fancy seaplane you got with the floats. You give us the cash *and* that plane. That's the deal. Then you get the girl."

"Where?"

"You'll know soon enough. I'll text you the coordinates when we're ready."

"You hurt her, you'll die, Halcón. Know that."

"Think you're in a place to make threats?"

"Not a threat. Just a promise. I'll do whatever you want. But you'll hold up your end or wish like hell you had."

Chris was shaking beside me, fists clenched.

"We'll talk soon, Jardinero. I see a single cop, she dies."

The call ended.

I lowered Harper's phone and stared at it.

"They have her," Chris said. "Those bastards have her."

"We'll get her back."

"What do they want?"

I told him.

"Why your plane?"

"These guys run drugs. They'll add it to their fleet for a while. Till customs catches on and they abandon it. Sounded like they were in a car still. Maybe they're headed for an airport."

"Harper has to be terrified right now." Chris held his hands to his forehead. "If we give them what they want, will they give her back?"

They wouldn't. As soon as I showed up with the cash, they were going to kill her and me and take the money and the plane and go. But I wouldn't tell him that.

"We're going to get her back, Chris. Or die trying."

But right now, dying trying was the most likely option.

THIRTY

LIMBO

THE WORLD WAS dimmer driving back to the boat. The moon was out but my mood was dark.

Chris kept the motor at half-throttle and it took us nearly twice the time for our return trip. I suspected he was dreading telling Ava our discovery.

The helplessness was the worst part.

I'd been careless. Cavalier.

Ava and Chris deserved the majority of the responsibility for our circumstances, but I wasn't blameless. I'd stirred the hornet's nest confronting the two thugs on Johnny's lawn. Now Harper was paying for it.

Cassidy's eyes went wide when she let us in the sliding door at the back of the *Midlife Crisis*. Harper's absence said enough.

I told them what we'd found.

Ava listened with a hand over her mouth, eyes unblinking until she sank to her knees on the rug and broke down. Chris went to her and held her shoulders as she sobbed.

Cassidy forced back tears too as she attempted to comfort her sister, but held it together enough to ask the tough questions. Like what on earth we'd do now.

"We have to decide if we risk the involvement of the police," I said. "Personally, I vote no."

"The police have more resources. Maybe they'd find her faster?" Cassidy asked. "Amber alerts, more people looking?"

"These men said they'd kill her. I think they'll follow through."

"We'll give them what they want," Chris insisted. "No cops."

Ava's voice sounded hollow. Still in shock. "When will they call?"

"I suspect they'll phone again once they have a drop location set up. Where's the money?"

Chris stood and spoke for them. "It's in the back of a rental car. I parked it near the boat ramp at Coffee Pot Bayou tonight. Once I had Harper and Ava we were going to drive it to the plane."

"A rental car."

"I used the fake passport and a prepaid credit card for the rental. Coffee Pot is a nice neighborhood. We didn't know what else to do with it."

"Okay. We'll pick up the car like you planned, but take it to Whitted. They said they wanted me to bring the Stationaire wherever this meeting place is, so we can load the money into it. Meeting place could be a lake for all we know." I picked up my phone and checked my messages. "I want to make one call first."

The marina still had an old payphone near the entrance for some unknown reason, and today I was grateful. I fed it quarters and dialed the number Landon had called me from. It rang several times and I got an automated message telling me voicemail hadn't been set up yet. I hung up and swore. But I waited. Three minutes, Then five. I'd almost given up when the payphone rang. I picked up.

"It wasn't my idea," Landon said.

I ran a hand up my forehead and clenched my fingers in my hair. "Tell me she's okay."

"She will be for now. I'm making a play here. I've told them you're an asset, and hurting the girl will ruin any chance at something more profitable. Best thing for her is if you play ball."

"What kind of asset?"

"La Reina Tigre is a businesswoman. I told her you might be willing to fill the role Johnny left vacant. Acquire assets for her."

"You offered her Archangel?"

"She's still interested. The Angel name carries some weight down here. But you've got to prove yourself. She wants one of your planes as a joining fee, and her money back of course. You make a deal to work with her, you get the girl back alive."

"This how she expects to get my cooperation? Kidnap someone anytime we have a problem?"

"I'm trying to save your life, little brother. The girl's too. This is the play."

"First you try to buy Archangel out from under me, now I'm supposed to give it up to her for free. Some deal maker you are."

"These people have a lot of leverage, Bogey. And they aren't afraid to use it."

"If this Reina Tigre is a businesswoman, she knows kidnaping an American kid is anything but low-key. This gets out and it's international news."

"She'll value your discretion."

I took a tighter grip on the handset. "Where's Harper?"

"Okay, look. I shouldn't be telling you this, but they're bringing her here."

"To Mexico?"

"Los Tigres are getting out before the heat comes. Taking the girl wasn't anyone's idea of a great move, but it's happened and they're not going to back down. They're rigging the board in their favor. Keeping all the pieces close."

"Where?"

"They chose Scorpion Reef. You'll rendezvous there, make the swap, and bring a few other things back with you."

"A smuggling run? You're joking."

"Told you, you gotta prove yourself. You make the run, deliver the goods safely, she knows she can trust you."

"In my plane?"

"One of ours."

I pressed my knuckles into the wall next to the payphone. This deal kept getting worse the longer I stayed on the phone.

"What's the meeting time?"

"They're going to text you details and coordinates. Probably the girl's phone. I gotta go. Things are moving here."

"She's eleven years old, Landon. She's innocent of all this. And you're a piece of shit."

"I know."

He hung up.

And that was it. My life choices had dwindled down to two options: Join Landon in his world or let Harper die. And that was no choice.

Twenty years of fleeing my family's legacy. Now it was clear the track I'd run had been a circle. I was right back where I'd started.

If there was a way out, I couldn't see it.

I punched the wall and went back to the boat.

THIRTY-ONE

FLIGHT PLAN

"I'M GOING WITH YOU," Cassidy said.

"Like hell you are."

She was down in my cabin where I was packing a few things in an overnight bag.

"It's five hundred nautical miles to Scorpion Reef. You're exhausted. You need another pilot."

"This won't be safe. I can't put any more people at risk."

"Luke, it's not your decision alone."

"My plane, so I'm making it my decision."

"Harper needs us, Luke. She's the priority. It only goes better with better options. Four hours over the gulf in a Stationaire is a long haul, and you falling asleep at the controls does no one any good."

"Getting you into trouble doesn't help either."

"Our niece has been kidnapped. We do whatever it takes to get her back. So you need to stop declining my help and tell me how we're making this happen."

I sighed and weighed the options.

"I've been to Scorpion Reef as a kid. My bet is they'll be on

Isla Pérez. There are few buildings out there. A lighthouse. Wouldn't be the first time drug runners have used the place. But the setup is all in their favor."

"Mexican drug enforcement has to know it's an issue."

"If La Reina Tigre has as much cash as it seems, I'm doubtful they won't have DEA agents paid off in advance. But it's secluded out there. I'm betting they get in and out quickly either way. Long haul by boat, so we can't count on help from any locals."

"Airstrip?"

"Not unless they've got a big enough sand bar. I'm guessing that's why they are using seaplanes."

"You know what they want you to smuggle back for them?"

"Not yet. But cocaine is a good bet. That's the typical flow. Guns go south, drugs come north."

"So what's our move?"

"We don't have one."

She put a hand on her hip. "That's bullshit."

"Even if you came, that's two of us against an unknown number of cartel guys. What could we do?"

"You haven't faced worse? How do we even the odds?"

She cocked an eyebrow. Never one to accept excuses.

I thought for a moment, then picked up my phone and texted Reese.

>>> I need your trigger finger.

Reese only made it twenty seconds into my explanation.

"I'm in." She'd driven to the marina the second I told her about Harper. The clock on the oven read 11:00 now. Chris and Ava were down in the guest quarters on the far side of the boat so it was only three of us in the living room leaning over the chart of the gulf I'd set on the coffee table. Reese studied the distance. "How do we execute this?"

"Still working that out," I said. "My guess was that El Halcón will get clear of the US with Harper by daylight. Depends on where they fly out. Probably report back to mainland Mexico and La Reina Tigre, wherever these guys are based. They'll rally to the drop-off from there. Tomorrow afternoon maybe? Could be later. Time is theirs to control. This could be a long situation."

"What are our assets?"

"Few. We'll be taxiing up to a dock full of cartel guys with guns. Them holding Harper hostage somewhere on the island. Us in plain sight. We'll be sitting ducks on a dock. It's a tactical nightmare."

Reese crossed her arms and frowned. "We need to change some of the factors, but they're controlling all of them."

"Not necessarily," Cassidy argued. "With Landon's tip about the location, it gave us extra time. How do we exploit that?"

"It's not nothing," Reese said.

"They'll probably expect you to come through near Cancún, clear customs, and refuel." Cassidy traced the route with her finger.

"I could make Scorpion Reef direct in the Stationaire. It's got an extended fuel tanks mod, so probably enough fuel to make Mérida after."

"Do they know that?" Reese asked.

She and I shared a look. "No. That's a good point. They've only ever seen the plane from shots Johnny took. If they looked it up, it would only show the old listing from before I bought it. It had standard tanks then, so they couldn't know about the alteration."

"They'd believe it's going to take you a lot longer to get there than it will," Cassidy said. "More time."

"How do we weaponize time?" I asked.

Reese pointed to Scorpion Reef. "We get there first."

I didn't hate that.

"First problem," I said. "They won't like the idea of their millions in cash going through a customs checkpoint. Even if it won't be in reality, we'd need a plausible reason they'd think we could pull that off."

"Send them a picture of me in my airline captain uniform," Cassidy said. "Tell them I know the customs guys in Cancún, which I actually do. I might even have a picture with a couple of them. Promise them I can get it through with no hassles."

"They'll be skeptical, but let's say they buy that. Problem two. They'll track the Stationaire's registration number on Flight Aware or some other means. They'll know where it's going unless we keep the transponder off. And they'll know we wouldn't get into Cancún that way."

We all stared at the map a few seconds, then Reese put up a hand. "What if we used two planes? Swapped the transponders. One goes the way they expect. One goes direct." She drew it on the map.

I looked at the route. "A decoy."

"We don't have a second Stationaire," Cassidy said.

"No. But we've got something close." I leaned down the stairs to the guest berths. "Chris, you down there?"

A moment later he popped into view, rubbing at his eyes. "Yeah, Luke. What's up?"

"You said you wanted to fly your 210 to the Caribbean. I've got a change of plans for you. You're going to Mexico."

He blinked. "To get Harper back?"

"Sort of. Best chance we have."

He nodded. "Okay. Yeah. I'm in. Whatever it takes."

"We'll need the plane soon."

"I'll go get it."

I went back to Reese and Cassidy. "We have a second plane." I put my hands on my hips. "Next item."

"Shit ton of guns?" Reese suggested.

"Yeah."

"I can help with that."

What other women might spend on vacations or jewelry, Reese spent on her gun collection, so I knew she wasn't exaggerating.

"You'll have the hardest part of this," I said. "They'll expect me to show up in the Stationaire. Only way that works is we drop you at the island, then go refuel the plane and hide out till the drop. We come back pretending it's the first time and pray you've given us some kind of tactical ace up our sleeve."

"Like Magnum would."

She was making light of the situation, even knowing it was going to be hairy. But I knew not to question her resolve.

"Study the latest satellite images of the island we can find. You might need cover for up to twenty-four hours."

"I'll get packing," Reese said. "Want me to bring the big guns?"

"Biggest you've got."

"If we're going to get there before the Tigres, we need to go soon," Cassidy said.

I checked my watch.

"We have one more problem," she added. "We'll need a safe place to hide the 206 and the cash while we wait for the actual rendezvous."

I considered the chart. "None of these other islands in the reef provide enough in the way of cover. We'll have to go to the mainland."

"No transponder, no flight plan. It'll be daylight. We can't just drop into Mérida and refuel."

"We'll have to scrounge up some fuel along the coast somewhere. But we'll worry about that when we get there."

She was clutching her elbows, anxiety evident, but gave me a nod. "We'd better get packing."

The chart on the table showed a lot of water between us and Mexico. It was going to be a long night.

THIRTY-TWO
PREFLIGHT

THE PLAN WAS in place and we got to work.

The most annoying part of the process was needing to lose our police tails from the marina. But it wasn't difficult. I left first, and took Reese's motorcycle. I didn't want the cops to have any question of who they were following. I cruised through the Grand Central District, chose a brewery on Fifth Avenue South, and walked straight through to the back. I then joined a pack of twenty-somethings scanning out electric scooters from a nearby rental corral and zoomed off with them for a jaunt down the Pinellas biking trial. That dumped me back downtown, and I was able to navigate my way to the back side of the university campus and cut through it to the airport.

It wouldn't be long till the cops cruised by my hangar looking for me, but shortly after I'd left the marina, Cassidy had departed in her rental. No one followed her.

While I was leading my surveillance team around Grand Central, she made for the airport and pulled out the plane. After fueling it, she stashed the Stationaire between two rows of T-hangars out of view from the street. If the cops came onto the airport, there was no hiding the floatplane for long, but we only needed a short window.

Reese took my Jeep home to drop Murphy off, and to pick up her gear. At the same time she was drawing attention with my Jeep in the parking lot, Chris and Ava idled out of the marina in their boat. They took it to Coffee Pot Bayou to retrieve the rental car where they'd hidden the stolen cash. They had assignments to pick up supplies from there.

There was no way of knowing how Kara would take the news of Reese's plans, but they showed up together at the airport shortly after I did. Kara's expression was somber, but she helped unload Reese's tactical gear. There was a lot of it.

They embraced for a long time before Kara let go. Kara walked up to me with a glare. "She gets hurt, it's your fault."

"We'll keep her safe."

It was a lie and she knew it.

There was nothing safe about our plan.

But Reese looked as enthusiastic as I'd seen her since our Army days. A seasoned soldier has skills few civilians understand, and when the time comes to use them, it's best to stand back and let them do what they do best without interference. If Reese and Kara were going to survive as a couple, Kara would learn to understand that.

Cassidy set to work preflighting the plane while I removed the aircraft's transponder.

It was an unusual trade when Chris and Ava finally showed up. I gave Chris the Stationaire's transponder and the tool to install it in his Cessna 210. He gave me two satchels with millions in stolen cash and a new phone from Walmart with an international calling plan.

We also had two satellite phones I'd borrowed from the *Midlife Crisis*.

I hefted one of the satchels. "That's a lot of damn money."

"You really think this plan of yours will work?" Chris asked.

"As soon as you get the text from El Halcón, you pretend to think it over, then explain the route. Cancún. Then the reef. Transmit the photos of Cassidy if they need them. Give them every assurance they're getting their money back as fast as we can give it to them."

"What if they insist on talking to you? Or Cassidy."

"El Halcón specifically said he was going to text the info to Harper's phone. Let's hope that's what happens. If not, you bullshit him."

"I don't want to mess it up."

I rested a hand on his shoulder. "You got this. Take your plane. Fly the route as we discussed. We'll try to be in touch when you land. Then you can swap the transponders back, refuel and fly home. Numbers in the phones?"

He held up his new phone. "Yeah. Programed in like you said."

"We'll be out of range for a while, but keep the faith." I gave him a slap on the shoulder.

Ava hadn't said much since I'd first outed her plan at the boat. But she approached me now.

"You two have my daughter's life in your hands." She nodded toward Reese who was checking the action on one of her weapons.

"We'll do everything in our power to get her back."

"There's no part for me in this plan. Just sit and worry."

"You're our point of contact. If Chris and I can't get ahold of each other in Mexico, we'll call you. Come tomorrow morning, the police are going to get curious why Cassidy and I have up and disappeared, but you'll have to fend them off one more day."

"And after that?"

"Then we bring Harper home safely and it doesn't matter what the cops know."

"What am I supposed to tell them?"

"The truth might be a good idea. But not till we have Harper back."

"The truth," she repeated. "The truth that I'm a criminal, or that I'm a terrible mother who endangered my child." Her hand was trembling.

"This isn't the end of the story," I said. "We don't know how it shakes out."

"Bring Harper back to me, Luke. I won't survive if you don't."

For the first time in a lot of years, I gave Ava Carter a hug I didn't hold back from. And she looked like she needed it.

Chris and Ava watched us climb into the floatplane. We taxied to runway 18 with only the red light of the closed control tower gleaming down at us.

The rumble of the engine filled the cockpit with a sense of inevitability, and as the plane lifted clear of the runway without a transponder, we broke the first of what would be many flight rules.

I kept the plane low over the water, well beneath Tampa's Class B airspace, more of a danger to boats than other planes.

With the lights off we were soon a blur in the night to anyone trying to place the sound of the engine. We skimmed the surface of the bay all the way around Pinellas Point and out to the gulf. I considered flying under the span of the Skyway Bridge, but didn't want to risk the plane's registration number being caught on bridge suicide prevention cameras. I buzzed over the flat southern length of the bridge instead, and out into the dark open water beyond.

"You should get some rest," Cassidy said, laying a hand on my arm.

I met her eye and relinquished my hold on the controls.

She was already flying left seat. She checked our altitude and kept us below a hundred feet.

It was going to be a long and dangerous ride at this altitude, but it was nothing she couldn't handle. She even had a slight hint of a smile on her face as she settled into her heading. This type of flying was a far cry from cruising the flight levels in an airliner.

For the first hour my nerves were too amped to rest. Reese and I worked though the gear she'd need to take ashore on Isla Pérez, and pored over the few images of the island we'd been able to download from the Internet before the flight. But before long, Reese was fading. She settled into a more comfortable position in the back seat and slept.

Out the window, moonlight on the glistening water of the gulf flashed beneath the pontoons. The horizon was vague and ominous. But Cassidy had a steady hand on the controls, alert for trouble.

There was only one guarantee in our plan, and finding trouble was it.

THIRTY-THREE
ENROUTE

CASSIDY WOKE me thirty minutes from Scorpion Reef.

The moon had set sometime after I'd nodded off.

Cass looked tired.

"Want me to take the controls?"

"Please. I just need to stretch."

At a hundred feet we weren't skimming the surface but still low enough to not be picked up by Cancún approach control radar. I descended even lower as we approached the coordinates for the reef.

Reese stirred as well and sat up. She started applying face paint from an Army issue camouflage stick. "Anyone bring any coffee on this trip?"

Cassidy reached under her seat and extracted a can of iced espresso she'd been keeping in a cooler pack beneath her legs. She handed it back to Reese.

Reese took it and read the label. "Oh, shit. You actually did."

"There are different levels of survival gear," Cassidy said. She popped another top and handed me a can too.

"Didn't know this plane had in-flight service."

But our moods grew somber again as we neared our destination.

Scorpion Reef sat sixty-seven nautical miles north of the Yucatan peninsula. The atoll had five islands large enough to support vegetation, but only Isla Pérez had habitations on it. I'd plotted our course to come up south of the island—which necessitated burning extra fuel—but we'd be downwind so the sound of the engine wouldn't carry as well to anyone who happened to be on the island.

There was a good chance there wouldn't be more than a couple residents around. I had memories of a lighthouse keeper and the occasional day-tripping fishing charter tourists, but of the half dozen buildings on the island, several were dilapidated and not fit for use. Visitors typically had to sleep on their boats.

Reese and I hoped one of the outbuildings might serve as cover for her to post up in, or under, for however many hours it would take till the rendezvous. But she had a ghillie suit too and could blend into the ground cover if the situation among the buildings was too exposed.

The beacon from the lighthouse was clearly visible as we turned north and headed for the southern tip of the island. The seas were calm so I landed a quarter mile from shore and plowed forward at a little more than idle speed. When we approached the southern beach, Cassidy took the controls while I climbed out onto a pontoon to assist the water rudders with an oar. Reese exited the other side, but instead of an oar, she kept her M4 carbine aimed at the shrubbery on the beach.

Cassidy cut the engine completely and we surfed the plane ashore in gentle waves until we ran aground. I hopped off with an anchor line and secured us, then returned to help with the gear as Reese kept her weapon ready. Cassidy and I made short work of offloading the items Reese would soon carry.

She had a MK 20 sniper system with sixty rounds, along with two hundred rounds of ammunition for the M-4. With a sidearm, plus food, water, and her body armor, two claymores, and the smoke and fragment grenades, it was a heavy load. I moved with her along the beach carrying some of it as we scanned the terrain ahead. The first hints of daylight were starting to appear on the Eastern horizon so the clock was ticking. If anyone was awake, they weren't moving around yet. Reese donned the ghillie suit while I kept watch, then we used the vegetation as concealment and skirted the beachhead around to the east.

"Okay. I'll need to get scouting for a spot to post up," she said. "I think I can hump all this stuff from here."

"You run into trouble. Shoot everybody."

When she had all of her other gear situated, I handed her the beast of a gun that was the MK 20 and the sat phone.

"You don't come back, my ass is cooked, so I might as well."

"I'll be back. Hell or high water."

Her face was covered in paint and shrouded by the suit, so it was hard to make out her expression, but she held up a fist and I bumped it. We held it a moment longer than usual, but then broke apart. She jogged twenty yards and vanished into the vegetation.

I swallowed hard and reminded myself this wasn't her first rodeo. Then I headed south again, my Sig Sauer sweaty in my hand.

Cassidy blew out a breath when she saw me and lowered her pistol by a few degrees. Her flight deck officer training had made her proficient in carrying a firearm, but there was a long way between defending a flight deck from a hijacking and getting in a firefight on a beach. She climbed quickly back into the 206 as I stowed the anchor and pushed us free of the sand.

I paddled us as far downwind as I could in the five minutes

we'd allotted, then Cassidy started the engine and got us moving away from the island.

Darkness was receding, and we were in view of the island's lighthouse now, so I said a silent prayer that the lighthouse keeper wasn't an early riser.

We got the Stationaire up on plane and departed the surface, maintaining our southerly heading. Once we were level at fifty feet and had the elevator trimmed, Cassidy finally turned in her seat to look back at the island. "You as worried about her as I am?"

"Can't be right now. Won't help her any." I checked the battery on my satellite phone anyway.

She nodded and faced the instrument panel. "Fuel's getting low."

I turned the fuel tank selector so it would feed from only the right tank and checked my watch. Once the engine started to sputter, I'd switch back to the left tank and know roughly how much time we had to work with before it would quit.

"You said you'd come up with a plan," Cassidy pressed.

"Here." I pointed to the coastline showing on the GPS. I programmed in the waypoint. "It's a spring at the coast called El Cenote Eletepén. It's remote. Some occasional hikers. We dock there until we find fuel. There's a pueblo not far by boat, but we may have to hoof it to find gas if no one is around."

"You think this thing will run okay on Mexican auto gas?"

"'Okay' might be the best we can hope for. But it'll work till it doesn't."

The engine coughed ten miles from the shoreline, and I quickly switched tanks before it could quit.

"Final reserve," I said, and checked my watch. "It'll get us to the scene of the crash at least."

But the mouth of the coastline appeared ahead of us on

schedule. Cassidy did the landing this time, flaring the 206 gently till the pontoons kissed the surface. She kept us on step till the color of the water changed, then let off the throttle and plowed toward the dock. The water was clear green here. The dock was quiet, and in the morning light, it could have made a scene for a tropical postcard. We cut the engine and glided up amid the cawing of seabirds.

I jumped off the pontoon and tied us off. There was a new sign for the place, but no boats or anyone to greet us. I guessed Monday morning wasn't a popular time for swimmers seeking freshwater sinkholes.

"Stay here while I scope things out."

"Why do I get guard duty?"

"Quién de nosotros puede hablar más español?"

"What? Shit. Okay, fine."

"I'll have a look around and see if anyone is here."

But there wasn't.

The dock had been rebuilt recently, some of the boardwalk path to the springs had been repaired too, but after a short walk along the walking path it was clear we were alone. I walked back to the dock.

"If we don't see any boats in the next few minutes, I may need to hike out to the road, or I could try the shoreline route."

Cassidy squinted into the rising sun, then turned the other direction to scan the horizon. The water was quiet. "We're exposed out here."

"There's an inlet to the east. Place called Boca de Islote. If you run into trouble, you can hide the plane there if need be."

"You taking the sat phone?"

"Keep it here. I don't want to risk Reese's only lifeline. I'm getting decent reception on my cell. I'll call you if I run into trouble."

Cassidy looked uneasy, but there was nothing else for it. We weren't getting anywhere without gas.

So I left my ex-wife, my plane, and the millions in cash that I needed to save my only niece floating alone at a dock in the middle of nowhere.

THIRTY-FOUR
ALMOST PARADISE

THIS STRETCH off the Yucatan coast was far removed from the tourist meccas of Cancún and Cozumel. The path I was on was a hiking trail of red clay that led me to a rutted road made of the same stuff. I set a pin on my new phone to note my location, but I scratched at a tree with my pocket knife also, to mark where I'd come out of the foliage. I was a believer in having a backup plan for when technology fails.

It had to be at least ninety degrees out and my shirt stuck to me. I walked another mile before I spotted signs of civilization and that was only an abandoned house, the roof long gone and the four walls left to be reclaimed by the jungle.

After another quarter mile I hit a paved stretch. It was still remote, the concrete stained nearly as red as the clay road had been. A stray dog trotting along the road the opposite direction gave me a wide berth. But after I didn't harass it, it seemed to reconsider its destination and began to follow me. After fifteen minutes of walking, a battered blue pickup truck appeared on the road behind me. I'd acquired a trail of three stray dogs at this point. Two men sat in the cab of the truck while a third rode in the truck bed. They slowed and the passenger leaned his head out.

"Necesitas ayuda?"

I most definitely did need help, so I walked up to the truck. My Spanish came out a little slower now than it had when I was kid, but they didn't seem to mind.

"Is there gas nearby?"

"Where is your car?"

"I'll need a lot. Three hundred and fifty liters."

The guy whistled and turned to his friend. They conversed and the driver said. "We have a friend with a big tank in his truck. He could get some gas in Cansahcab."

"I'll need to bring it to the waterfront. I need it at dock near here."

They conversed a bit longer, then the passenger turned to me. "We were on our way to Santa Clara. But, we could help."

"I'm happy to pay you for your time. All three of you. And your friend with the tank."

That must've given them the positive motivation they needed. The guy in the passenger seat got out and offered me his seat. I thanked him and he climbed into the back of the truck bed with the third man. Maybe whatever was waiting in Santa Clara wasn't a sure payday. Whatever the case, I had myself a crew.

We bumped along for twenty minutes before reaching the nearest town. It bore the name Dzilam de Bravo Municipality. A mouthful. But the town was home to a couple thousand people so it hosted a handful of restaurants, hotels, and bars. The waterfront was a sandy dirt road lined with coconut palms and low, sun-bleached, concrete houses. But it had what I needed, easy street access to a variety of docks. It would do.

I indicated the dock I wanted. "This will work here. I have a friend going to show up here. How long to get the gas?

There was some confusion about why I wanted it at a dock.

"You don't need marine gas?"

"No. Auto gas. Highest octane you can get. Ninety-three octane. Not the eighty-seven."

I actually wanted one hundred octane avgas, but I was being realistic.

"It's not a boat?"

"It's a plane." I pulled out my wallet and extracted five one hundred-dollar bills. "Three-hundred-and-fifty liters of gas. Ninety-three octane. I'll give you each another two hundred dollars for your trouble when I get it."

The guys chattered a bit and got excited. I was guessing they didn't see a lot of seaplanes, or hundred dollar bills. Finding out I was a pilot seemed to improve their trust in me.

They estimated it would take an hour to get the truck with the tank. Another forty minutes to get to the Pemex in Cansahcab. Round trip I was looking at three hours. If they vanished with my five hundred dollars, I'd never see them again and would be worse off than I'd started. But I got a responsible vibe from Ernesto, the driver. The promise of making another two hundred dollars each was a good payday.

There was some concern as to whether I had the cash, expressed from the guy in the back, but Ernesto hushed him. Maybe he got a responsible vibe from me too. Whatever the case, we exchanged contact numbers and left me at the dock with assurances they'd be back in three to four hours with my gas.

It was a gamble, but despite some evidence I'd run into over the years, I believed that most people were inherently honest. Or at least wanted to be. I'd find out in three to four hours.

After scouting the dock, I walked down the dusty street till I found a house that also advertised itself as an internet cafe. The cafe was basically someone's living room made up into a makeshift coffee shop with a couple of ten-year-old computers. But it had Internet access and that was good enough for me.

Flight Aware was slow to load, but when I entered my aircraft's registration number, a flight track showed the aircraft currently enroute to Cancún. By my estimation, it had less than an hour to go.

I rested easier knowing Chris had successfully installed the transponder. But the tricky bit was yet to come.

I called Cassidy next and filled her in on my progress.

"I had a call from Ava," she said. "El Halcón texted the destination. Isla Pérez like your brother said. They want us there this afternoon. They weren't happy about Cancún."

"It's possible La Reina Tigre has people there. Good chance they'll try to grab the cash at the airport."

"How pissed off will they be when they don't get it?"

"As long as we have it, and they don't, Harper is going to be okay."

"I'm scared for her, Luke."

"You and me both."

I sent her the location of the dock where I planned to meet. "Just get the plane here when I call you. We've got this."

"If your gas doesn't show up, we'll be stuck there permanently."

"It'll show."

She hung up and I wandered out to the water and took a seat on a concrete wall beneath a palm tree. A few old boats lay at anchor. If it wasn't for the weight of the gun under my shirt and the knot of worry in my stomach, the place could have passed for paradise.

I told myself I had everything under control.

But I was a lousy liar.

THIRTY-FIVE
FUEL STOP

I'D JUST CHECKED my watch for about the hundredth time in the last three hours when a phone rang in my pocket. I had two of them now and it took me a moment to figure out which was ringing.

Landon was on the other end when I picked up.

"What game are you playing, Bogey?"

I kept my eyes on the distant horizon.

"Just following the plan you gave us, brother. Selling my soul to the devil."

"Tread carefully. There are some hot tempers around here. Some say you may not be playing by the rules."

"Made it to Mexico, if that's what you're asking. Money is safe. We're in-country and on our way to Scorpion Reef shortly."

"What happened in Cancún?"

"No problems."

"Rumor is no one saw a floatplane land this morning."

"Maybe La Reina Tigre needs better informants."

He stayed quiet for several long seconds. When he spoke again, his voice was low. "There ain't but a couple ways out of this situation, Bogey. I can't say you're gonna love any of 'em. But I prefer the one where you fly home safe. You know that."

"Excuse me if my trust in you isn't at an all-time high."

"You want to tell me where you are right now?"

"Nope."

"Anything happens to that money, you know it goes bad for that little girl."

I tightened my grip on the phone but kept my tone controlled. "How is she?"

"Le Reina Tigre is fit to be tied."

"*Harper*, Landon."

"I've seen her. She's okay. For now. I'll see you in a few hours, little brother. Let's see this thing all the way through."

When he hung up, I didn't take my eyes off the horizon.

I was waiting on the dock when Ernesto and his buddies returned. He hadn't been joking about the fuel tank. It looked to be about five hundred gallons in capacity. Bad news was it had a hand cranked pump. But beggars can't be choosers.

I texted Cassidy and got an immediate reply.

The guy driving the fuel truck gave me a skeptical glance as they got it positioned, but all eyes went wide when the Cessna 206 flew into view and splashed down a hundred yards out. The looks of awe only grew when they saw it was a woman at the controls, and when Cassidy stepped out of the plane, all long legs, glowing skin, and hair blowing in the wind, a couple of the guys went weak in the knees.

We had to pull the plane all the way up the dock and beach it to get the truck's fuel hose to reach, but with a bit of ingenuity, we got pumping. The plane drew a crowd. That part wasn't ideal. Cassidy kept a wary eye out while she charmed the locals. Last thing we needed was extra attention.

I got the fuel hose in the right wing and Ernesto's guys started pumping. But just as we finished the first wing, a police car showed up.

I swore and quickly transferred the fuel nozzle over to the left wing.

"Come on, come on, come on," I muttered as the fuel got flowing again.

"I've got this," Cassidy said and walked toward the street, waving at the police officer and jogging to meet him.

As soon as the tank was full, Ernesto and his two friends helped me shove the pontoons off the beach and I pulled the plane along the dock to its farthest point.

Cassidy was doing an admirable job chatting up the police officer in apologetic English, smiling and playing the tourist and keeping him at a distance.

I paid Ernesto and he gave each of his guys their promised cash. But by now the police officer was nosing forward, gesturing to me. I waved, then busied myself in the plane, getting the controls set for a quick start.

The police officer walked out the dock, shouting something now and waving.

I ignored him.

Cassidy walked along with him, even going so far as to rest a hand on his forearm. But the officer was blatantly suspicious now. And a few members of the crowd of locals had taken an interest in the outcome too.

Last thing we needed was a delay. And as armed Americans with millions in cash in their plane, we were sitting on a powder keg of trouble.

I had the plane turned around now, nosed out, and I held it close to the dock by only one line.

"Come here, please," the cop shouted in Spanish.

"We're just leaving," I said. "Thanks for your help."

"No. No. Come here please. You need a permit. All planes at this dock need a permit."

I was confident no plane had ever visited this dock. There was good chance a small bribe could solve this problem, but I was fresh out of cash and wasn't about to go digging around in La Reina Tigre's duffle bags for a bribe for this guy.

He had a hand resting on his gun now and approached with more tenacity.

"Yes. Permits. Of course." I smacked a palm against my forehead. "How much is the permit?" I held my ground, making an excuse of the line I was holding.

"Tie that back up," the cop demanded. "You come with me."

Cassidy and I shared a glance. Her jaw was set.

"How about you hold this for me while he and I talk," I said in English, offering her the line.

"I think I have this, babe. You trust me?"

"Do what you think is best."

She turned and kicked the cop in the back of his knee. He shouted in alarm as she put all her weight into the guy with both hands, shoving him toward the edge of the dock. The cop yelped as he flailed, trying to regain his balance. He teetered and went over the edge. I rushed forward and caught Cassidy's arm, just as she was in danger of going over too. The cop hit the water with a gigantic splash and a shout of amazement from the onlookers. Someone laughed.

When the cop came back up, he was sputtering and shouting between mouthfuls of seawater. Looked like he could swim though.

"Adios, amigos," I shouted to Ernesto and his buddies. Then Cassidy and I scrambled into the 206 the fastest I've ever gotten into a plane.

The engine fired up immediately. I would've liked to take time to sump the fuel tanks and do more diligence, but another police car had arrived at the beach and this cop got out with a gun drawn.

I advanced the throttle and plowed out through the light waves, gaining speed and waiting each moment for the report of gun fire. If it came, it didn't matter. We had the floats on-plane and were skipping over the waves now. I pulled back on the yoke and got airborne, banking low in small turns as we went, then climbing up and away out to sea.

Cassidy was watching behind us, but eventually turned her attention back to me. Her face was flushed. "Well, that's one more thing I've never done as an airline captain."

"You made a good bowling ball. Don't think he'll forget you."

"Learned it from one of Ava's Krav Maga videos. We're in big trouble now, huh?"

"Nothing we can't handle."

She put her sunglasses on and looked out the passenger side window, but her left hand found mine on the throttle control and she left it there, her fingers interlaced with mine.

THIRTY-SIX

ANGELS COLLIDE

SIXTY MILES over water ought to have felt short after the distance we'd already covered, but each passing mile seemed to stretch. Cassidy climbed into the back seat to organize our things and checked the magazines on our remaining weapons. My stomach growled audibly so she passed me a granola bar. We were due at Isla Peréz, but our rushed departure from the mainland meant I wasn't ready yet. Not mentally, not tactically. But I had one more idea, so I put the 206 back in the water just off Isla Pájaros, an uninhabited coralline island on the extreme southern tip of Scorpion Reef.

"What are you doing?" Cassidy asked as I shut the engine down and popped the door open.

"You said we should do everything we can to improve our odds. So I'm making improvements."

Cassidy stayed in the cockpit while I climbed out to the left pontoon. My only tools were a spare T-shirt and a roll of white duct tape, but I got to wiping water off the pontoon under the front landing gear wheel.

"Hand me the Colt."

Cassidy passed the revolver out to me.

"I'm pretty sure we'll be searched the minute we get there." I ripped a piece of duct tape. "They'll want any guns we have on us."

"So we keep a few not on us?"

I shrugged. "I didn't say it was a great plan. But it's better than nothing."

"Then I want one too." Cassidy took off her shirt, revealing the bikini top she had on beneath, then climbed out on the other pontoon with a second pistol. She got to wiping in a similar location low down on the inside of the pontoon. I finished securing my Colt. The white duct tape blended in well with the white of the pontoon and under the amphibious gear, it was out of sight. I made sure the handle stuck out enough to grab, but it wasn't obvious.

I smiled and tossed Cassidy the duct tape.

We climbed back into the flight deck after and I restarted the engine. Isla Peréz was nearly visible on the horizon.

"I want you to promise me something," I said.

"Don't you dare give me one of your ultimatums right now."

"You know things might go badly. I just want to hear that if we get a chance to, you'll put Harp on this plane and go. With or without me, you get her out of there."

"We're all getting out together."

"That's plan A. But you getting Harper out solo is plan B."

"Would you leave *me* behind?"

I clenched my jaw. "No."

"Then don't give me your heroic male bullshit." Cassidy's expression was all determination. "And let's go get our girl."

"Yes, ma'am."

I pushed the throttle forward and got us airborne again.

Cassidy looked back over.

"You never once said 'Yes, ma'am' while we were married. Is this you maturing?"

"This is me not wanting to argue with the woman risking her life to be here with me."

Cassidy studied the horizon. "I'll get her out alone if I have to. But I won't like it."

"Never liked seeing you leave, myself."

The shallow water of the reef was iridescent beneath us. We passed a shipwreck from some unsuspecting sailor that ran aground and abandoned the craft in a tradition centuries old. Scorpion Reef had claimed a lot of souls.

The closer we got to Isla Pérez, the closer we were to joining them.

The dock near the lighthouse was occupied by one boat and one Cessna Grand Caravan on floats. The Caravan was docked close in, meaning I'd be forced farther out, a long walk under the watchful eye of whoever we were meeting. And as we splashed down over the coral beds, the first of our welcome committee came into view.

While I'd heard the island occasionally hosted Mexican Navy soldiers, I doubted many of them toted Kalashnikovs. The two guys that walked out the dock now wore low-slung shorts with their boxers visible. The shorter guy was shirtless, brandishing a chest of gang tattoos and had his pistol tucked in his pants. The guy with the Kalashnikov was tattooed as well but wore a backwards ball cap and a bandana with a skull on it over his face. I glided the 206 up to the dock and hopped out, making the leap across to the dock and guiding the aircraft by the wing strut. I snatched up a dock line and tied the plane off, then straightened to meet the two men. There were several more dudes near the buildings, watching. Maybe six of them. None I recognized.

"Dondé esta El Halcón?"

The guy with the Kalashnikov clutched it tighter to his chest and shouted back in Spanish. "You wait right there. Don't move. Lift up your shirt."

I lifted my shirt and turned slowly to show I wasn't carrying a gun.

"You get out," the little guy with no shirt said.

Cassidy met my eye from inside the plane, but climbed out. The short gangster took a step back and seemed to be considering searching her, but since she was only wearing jean shorts and her bikini top, he thought better of it. She was taller than him too and he looked intimidated.

Sometimes beauty is its own armor.

There was no sign of Harper. Or Reese for that matter. But I knew she'd be watching. I kept my head still, sunglasses concealing my efforts, but scanned the shoreline quickly. I wouldn't spot her—Reese was no amateur—but there were a couple of spots that looked likely as firing positions. I just hoped she had good line of sight to these assholes.

The reason for the wait became evident a moment later when I caught the distinctive sound of engines reverberating over the water. That was no Stationaire or Caravan. I knew even before I saw the aircraft that the sound came from two Pratt and Whitney Wasp Radial engines. I'd heard them enough times in my life that they'd become a core memory. And as the plane came into view around the north end of the island, gooseflesh prickled at my arms.

It was *Tropic Angel*.

Her paint was faded and the engine nacelles were stained with exhaust. A few dents lined the leading edge of the left wing, but it was the same plane. A resurrected ghost.

The Grumman Mallard dipped and did a low pass along the beach, buzzing the dock. The two goons with guns ducked as the flying boat roared a mere dozen feet over our heads.

Landon. Always the showman.

The plane banked left, flew out over the water in a wide teardrop turn then came back around to splash into the Gulf several hundred yards off the beach. It motored up with it's engines thrumming, the vibrations from the twin nine-cylinder engines reverberating through the wooden dock at my feet. Landon taxied the plane nearly to the beach, choosing a spot at the north side of the dock, but instead of docking, he extended the landing gear and gunned the engines, forcing the Mallard up the beach via the remnants of a submerged concrete ramp I hadn't previously noticed. The maneuver was loud and unnecessary, but it was flashy and testosterone fueled, so not shocking.

Amid the noise, Cassidy stepped out from under the wing of the 206 to have a better look at the Mallard. Imminent danger or not, a gorgeous plane was a gorgeous plane. And they didn't make planes like that one anymore.

The gangsters on the beach had chattered excitedly about the plane too, moving that way, but when Cassidy emerged into the sunlight, the attention of the two guys closest to us refocused. I didn't blame them. Things of beauty were plentiful around this dock at the moment. Not many like her had been made either.

Standing there with the sun on her tanned skin, I was hit with a pang of loss more acute than I'd felt in years. I thought I'd come to terms with our divorce a long damn time ago, but the last twenty-four hours had me wondering what kind of idiot I must have been to think I'd ever stop loving this woman. And now I'd put her in danger.

As the engines shut down, the hatch on the Mallard opened and the ladder extended. El Halcón was the first out, followed by his tank of a thug buddy I'd punched on Johnny's lawn. The next person out was Harper, dropped roughly out to the beach where she tripped but was caught by the big bald gangster. She spotted us when she regained her feet.

"Uncle Luke? Aunt Cass!"

She started to run toward us, but was grabbed by El Halón and spun around. "Not yet, chiquita." He snatched her arm with one hand, yanking her to him while he pulled a pistol with another. He passed her off to the bald guy who clamped her shoulders like a vise.

I clenched my fists.

El Halcón looked Cassidy over from a distance as he strode onto the dock. "I see you brought me more presents. I approve."

But before I could reply, a fourth person climbed out of the Mallard. He wore a floral shirt and a Panama hat with linen pants. His light beard had a few flecks of gray at the chin but otherwise he looked the same as he had ten years ago.

Landon Angel dropped off the last rung of the boarding ladder, set his hands on his hips, and smiled in my direction. He strolled onto the dock like this was a day at a yacht club.

"Glad you made it, Bogey. I always knew we'd end up back together like this one day. Hello, Cassidy." He gave her a nod. Then he stretched his arms wide and gestured to the island. "We live the life, don't we? To think there's suckers who will never know what this is like. Paradise."

"Strange place to meet the devil," I said.

He shook his head as he closed the distance. "Same old Luke. Too hung up on your issues to appreciate the finer things in life. I see why you ditched him, Cass."

Cassidy stepped up next to me. "Give me back my niece, Landon. Let's all fly out of here."

"That's the plan, darling. Just so long as Luke does as he's agreed."

"You got our money?" El Halcón shouted. "Let's see it."

The shirtless little guy with all the prison tats stepped around me and walked to the plane. Looked like he'd never seen a floatplane before.

"It's in the back," I clarified.

He took an unsteady step onto the pontoon and nearly fell. But he figured out the baggage door handle and pulled it open. He poked his head in.

"Sí, está aqui!"

"Get it out," El Halcón shouted.

I walked back to the plane to help.

"Hey, back off!" the little gangster shouted, hand on his pistol.

"They're heavy. You want to fall in the water getting them out, be my guest."

He grudgingly accepted that I was a lot bigger and stronger than he was. "Órale, you do it."

I hoisted the duffle bags out to the dock under his watchful supervision and he struggled to lift them onto his shoulders. Kalashnikov guy could've helped, but he didn't.

Little prison tats guy waddled back to El Halcón, teetering under the weight of the duffel bags on each shoulder, then dropped them at his boss's feet with a thud.

"Check it," the gangster ordered.

The little guy unzipped the satchels and rummaged around. There was no way he could count it all, but he checked both bags and nodded. "It's good."

"It's all there," I said. "Now give us Harper."

Harper moved to come toward us but El Halcón shook his head. "She stays. Till you do the run. This one too." He pointed to Cassidy. "Mamacita and I gonna get to know each other while you're gone."

"Go to hell," I said. "That wasn't the deal."

"You think you're in a place to make deals right now, pendejo?"

"This is business, Luis," Landon said. "Let's not make it difficult."

"Luis? Who you fucking calling *Luis*, guero? I'm *El Halcón*."

"We can all calm down, is all I'm saying," Landon suggested. "For the sake of the deal."

"You think, cause you been boning La Reina Tigre that makes you big shit? That don't make you nothing, cabrón. On this island, I'm the boss." He kicked one of the bags of money. "We got our shit back. We got the plane. You tell me what we need his stupid ass for?"

"This isn't the only plane we need," Landon said. "Luke has a legitimate business that will be a perfect fit for what we—"

"Fuck that," El Halcón interjected. "This guy knows too much. He knows we killed that Lamborghini guy. And he fucking hit my best dog. I don't stand for that shit. You want to hit my fucking dog, too?" He pointed his pistol at Landon. Landon put his hands up.

El Halcón had the whole dock frozen in place now.

He turned to the guy with the skull mask bandana and the Kalashnikov and pointed to me. "Nacho, kill that piece of shit."

Kalashnikov guy looked unsure only for a second, but then he hoisted the rifle and aimed at me. For some reason he pulled his mask down to aim and I got a better view of his tattooed face. He had a tear drop under one eye, and a number of other things I never got to see because the next moment the left side of his face went missing.

THIRTY-SEVEN
GUNS UP

THE REPORT of the MK 20 carried over the water a second behind the shot. That's why when Nacho lost his face and went spinning off the dock, it looked almost like he'd planned it. The eerie dance of his suddenly lifeless body being carried off the dock was a silent pirouette.

The second shot came close behind the sound of the first, catching the edge of El Halcón's left shoulder and making him shout in alarm.

Then all hell broke loose.

Getting shot at is always a jolt of adrenaline. Even when it's friendly fire.

El Halcón turned and ran, but not before grabbing Harper from his bald buddy and clutching her to him like a shield. He put his bleeding arm around her neck and pulled her along the dock behind him while she shrieked. Cassidy lunged to go after her, but the little gangster tats guy and El Halcón's bald henchman were still in our way. Baldy pulled his pistol and fired a couple of wild shots toward the beach, then turned and shot at us, missing, but close enough that a round whizzed past my ear.

The guys on the beach had erupted into action too, snatching guns and running around trying to figure out who was shooting. A couple picked up rifles and started shooting at my plane. A bullet went through the left wingtip of the Stationaire above me and I ducked and grabbed Cassidy's hand. We went off the back of the dock together, gracelessly, into the water behind the floatplane. It was just in time, it turned out, because the little prison tats guy had a sudden burst of courage and ran up behind us, firing into the water.

Cassidy and I stayed underwater, deep enough that the bullets from the young thug's pistol lost their potency, burbling through the water around us before sinking toward the sand a few feet beneath us. Cassidy and I shared a look and I pointed toward the front of the plane. She nodded, and we swam, surfacing once at the outboard side for air, then going under again to come up near the front of the pontoons.

I snatched the first pistol from under the landing gear and passed it to Cassidy, who was clutching the side of the right pontoon. I went under again and came up at the other pontoon, retrieving my Colt Python.

Prison tats guy saw me this time and shouted. I ducked back under the pontoon and swam beneath the surface till I was under the dock. A moment later Cassidy came up next to me. The guys above us were running around looking for us. I dumped the water out of the barrel of my Python and put two rounds through the dock above us, splintering wood and not hitting the guy, but it did scare the shit out of him.

"Pinche mierda!" he shouted. He fired randomly into the dock. By then Cassidy and I were both underwater again. I gave her a sign to stay put under the dock, then I swam back under the seaplane. The bald thug and the little guy were both using the plane as cover from Reese's shots from the brush. They'd figured out generally where she was, but didn't seem to be doing much with the information. I came up gently beneath the left pontoon of the seaplane, finding a grip with my left hand and quietly pouring water from the barrel of my Python with my right. I took one deep breath, then I used my left arm to heave myself up over the pontoon, at the same time leveling my my pistol at the dock. I got two shots off. The first hit Baldy in his right side. My second I went for the little guy, but he shrieked and moved. My shot only grazed his leg.

I caught more cursing before I went under again.

In the clear tropical water, I could easily make out Cassidy, lingering near one of the dock pilings still holding her breath beneath the surface. She'd always been even better at it than me and now she had added motivation. The water was only eight to ten feet deep here and she'd found the bottom with her deck shoes. A few bubbles escaped her lips but she was in no distress. I gave her a reassuring wave, then I surfaced again, this time in a different spot toward the rear of the plane. No one shot at me this time. I scanned the gaps between the boards above and saw a dark shape. Might have been Baldy. He didn't appear to be moving. I didn't see the little guy, and that bothered me.

"Eat this, fucker!" he suddenly shouted in English. An arm appeared out the open baggage door of the Stationaire. He fired wildly down at the pontoon near my head.

"Geezus," I blurted and lifted my gun. I put two quick shots through the floor of the plane's baggage area.

Then I went underwater again.

I gestured to Cassidy.

She swam over and I traded guns with her.

When we surfaced together toward the front of the plane this time, the world had gone quiet.

The shooting at the beach had calmed, everyone seeking cover.

I scanned the beachhead quickly, looking for any signs of Reese, but saw nothing.

Cassidy kept her gun pointed at the immobile dark lump on the dock.

"Is this thing still loaded?"

"Two rounds left in that one. Make 'em count."

I moved around to the inboard float and tried to get a look inside the open baggage door of the 206.

Cassidy and I shared a questioning look, but finally there was nothing else for it. I had to go up and check. I decided on the right outboard float as my way up. Reese was that direction. Arguably she might be able to provide cover, but it wouldn't help me from the guy inside the plane. I went for it anyway, rolling myself up onto the float in one swift motion and going for the passenger door handle. I swung the door open and stuck my head and the .38 in, not high, but looking low under the seats instead.

The guy was still back there, but he didn't move. Finally, I rose, carefully, debating just putting rounds through the seats.

But as I climbed up, I spotted the top of the young man's head, his hair matted with blood. He stared lifelessly back at me. One of the rounds I'd fired through the floor had come up through the bottom of his chin and out his left temple.

I looked away and swallowed down the threat of rising bile, then dared to peek out the left window to the dock where the prone form of the bald gangster lay. His shirt was stained red and he didn't appear to be breathing.

I let out a slow sigh and crouched to look for Cassidy. She'd come up for air behind the right Pontoon.

"They're both dead."

"What now?"

"I don't know."

I scrambled around the cabin of the plane, gathering our remaining weapons and ammo into the waterproof diving backpack I'd brought. I found the satellite phone and bagged that too.

A gunshot sounded from the north and I caught my first glimpse of Reese's position. She'd posted up on a grassy dune only a few hundred meters down the beach. For the MK 20 sniper rifle, that distance was nothing, but it was far enough away to reduce the risk from the small arms fire she was getting in return. The guys on the beach had scrambled for cover and were hiding in and around the scattered buildings. At least one body lay in view, prone on the ground with an AR style rifle in his hands. The guy had made the mistake of entering Reese's field of fire and paid the price.

She had the gangsters outgunned and I had minimal fears for her safety, except when I caught movement inside the top of the red-and-white striped lighthouse.

Sunlight glinted off the guy's watch.

Someone was up there.

As I looked on, the barrel of a rifle appeared over the parapet off the lighthouse. The guy was taking aim at Reese's position. Would she spot him in time?

From his angle, the shooter could fire over the dunes providing Reese's cover. The AR didn't have the precision accuracy of her sniper rifle, but it was still plenty deadly at that range.

I located my Sig Sauer, reopened the passenger door of the Stationaire and stuck my weapon out. This far away, I had slim chance of hitting the guy, but I could at least draw attention to him and warn Reese.

I squeezed off three quick rounds toward the top of the lighthouse. All three appeared to miss, so I took better aim and fired again, this time shattering a glass pane at the top of the beacon.

Gunfire erupted from the beach and the tink tink of bullets

ricocheted from the front cylinders of the 206. Another bullet came through the windshield.

"Shit," I blurted and ducked.

The last thing I saw before going out the door was the flash of the muzzle from Reese's position and erupting concrete at the top of the lighthouse.

Then bullets penetrated the fuel tanks of the 206 above me and my world exploded.

I hit the water face first, the blast above me obliterating all other sensations. I was vaguely aware of heat at my back, then I was underwater, the sea around me roiling and orange.

I could have been facing any direction. My sense of equilibrium was shattered. A moment of panic set in as I realized I was choking on seawater and nowhere near the surface.

Then I felt hands on me.

Cassidy pulled me toward her and we came up gasping beneath the flaming dock.

The 206 was still afloat somehow, but one of the wings was in the water. I blinked away my disorientation and a feeling of nausea as I watched the fuselage of my airplane burn. The explosion had ripped the top of the plane apart.

Bits of debris floated around us, but Cassidy shoved the dive pack she'd rescued into my arms and pulled me toward shore with her.

We stayed beneath the dock for cover, our small backpack of handguns and ammo feeling like a weak addition to this firefight. But it was a manageable enough weight to swim ashore beneath the dock.

As we passed under the dock, I noticed the dark shape of one of the duffel bags of money still sitting atop the boards. The second bag was missing. There was also no sign of Landon. Had he run ashore?

I supposed we'd find out soon enough.

When we reached the waist-deep water near the shoreline, I paused to catch my breath, then opened the backpack. Our arsenal was minimal. We had four handguns, of which two were revolvers with low ammo capacity. My Sig held fifteen rounds plus one in the chamber. Cassidy's pistol was a Glock 19 that likewise held fifteen, but neither was especially precise past twenty yards.

Our exit plan was now a smoldering wreck at the end of the dock. Our assets were rapidly dwindling.

I felt around my head.

Shit.

If we were going to storm this beach and get Harper back, we'd need a hell of a lot of luck.

And I'd already lost my lucky shades.

THIRTY-EIGHT
SHOWDOWN

THERE WAS an old wooden boat overturned on the beach, sunbleached paint flaking off into the tropical breeze. Someone had been working on patching it.

It got at least five more holes in it after Cassidy and I used it for cover.

We ran for a tiny statuary chapel next, Cass providing covering fire while I took point, then me blasting away at the closest outbuildings while she sprinted to catch up.

I had our pack slung over my back, a pistol in each hand. Cassidy held just the Glock she was most comfortable with. We were both sandy and scratched up. The Butch and Sundance vibes weren't lost on me. I just hoped our story ended better.

The Virgin Mary gazed down at us from her pedestal as I reloaded the Colt Python. Then the sat phone rang.

Cassidy yanked it from the backpack for me and handed it over.

"You just ran out of sight," Reese said, the moment I answered. "I'll need to move in thirty seconds."

I dared a look around the edge of the tiny chapel to the place Reese had been posted.

A couple of guys were creeping up from her right through the sparse trees, trying to flank her.

"You're going to have an opportunity for a distraction in about ten seconds," Reese added. "Take advantage."

Then the call ended.

"She okay?" Cassidy asked.

"Be ready."

We were both soaking wet and oozing water from our shoes, but our blood was pumping. Nothing like a gunfight to remind you you're alive.

The cartel guys working through the trees were only about a hundred and fifty meters from Reese. Then the explosion came—one of her claymore mines planted less than twenty meters ahead of them. They never knew they were dead.

I ducked behind the chapel as fragments of the mine danced off the roofs of nearby buildings.

Then we ran.

Men shouted in low buildings to our right and more gunfire erupted in Reese's direction. She'd thrown at least one smoke grenade, covering her exit.

If I knew anything about anything, she'd retreat to the north, then swing around from the northwest. So I went west too, hoping to pinch our remaining adversaries in the buildings between us.

One timeless move in a gunfight: don't be where they think you are.

In the chaos of the explosion, Reese had bought us concealment again.

The building we were hiding behind now was a dilapidated old structure that once housed the lighthouse keeper. One too many hurricanes had battered it, and it now teetered on the edge of collapse. Cassidy kept her gun pointed at the barracks building south of us, covering our six. We used our ears as much as our eyes, tuned for sounds of trouble.

The chattering I heard was coming from the far side of the same building we were hiding behind in a courtyard space between the other low buildings. The base of the lighthouse occupied the northwest corner of the little compound.

Their group was down at least five men. I hoped that was affecting their morale.

"What's your plan?" Cassidy whispered.

"Probably shoot all these guys."

"We only need Harper. If you were the guy that has her, where would you go?"

She had a point. If I was a shithead bad guy like El Halcón, I probably wasn't going to linger around the middle of a firefight and endanger my only hostage. He knew we wanted her. He'd keep that bargaining chip close and secure.

The lighthouse was an option. Damned thing was a tiny fortress, small windows and only one way in.

Or he ran clear across the island to the dock on the other side. A boat maybe?

"We still have to deal with these guys first," I said, gesturing toward the sound of heated Spanish chatter coming from the courtyard.

Her lips formed a thin line, but she nodded.

"Don't worry. We've got this." I crept forward, guns up, around the edge of the old house. There were only four remaining Cartel guys in view. One had a rifle, but three were only armed with small handguns. A couple were young, not much more than teenagers. The two older guys were shouting at them.

Then I spotted a welcome sight. Reese was approaching

through the trees from the northwest, her M4 Carbine at the ready. I signaled my intentions to her and she nodded.

I came around the corner and into the courtyard ready to start shooting, but one of the young guys spotted the movement. To my surprise, he immediately tossed his gun away and threw up his hands.

"Nos rendimos! Nosotros nos rendimos!"

Surrender. That was surprising.

His three companions swung around to spot me, but they looked unsure also.

"On the ground!" Reese shouted, emerging from the trees in her full camo and M4.

I translated to Spanish for the cartel guys and one-by-one, they slowly laid down their weapons and got on the ground, their eyes mostly on Reese. I didn't blame them. In the ghillie suit she looked like *Swamp Thing*.

"How many others?" I asked. "Where's the rest of you?"

One of the older guys shook his head vigorously. "No hay. Somos todos."

"And El Halcón?"

Two guys pointed toward the western beach. One just put his hands up farther.

"Now what?" Reese asked as she shed her ghillie suit into a pile on the ground.

Having our own hostages wasn't part of the plan, but it was going to have to be now.

And it was going to slow us down.

"You bring zip ties?" I asked.

"Nope."

"I can cover them," Cassidy said. "You two get Harp."

I collected the men's guns. Two of the pistols were spent. Even the rifle was empty. No wonder they'd surrendered.

They'd been packing the guns mostly for show. Gangsters, not soldiers. Unprepared for a true gunfight.

There was a big difference between talking a good game on the street and facing battle. I doubted they'd be scared straight, but I was guessing they'd bring more ammo next time.

There was a metal cistern in the courtyard. It had a lid on it wide enough to fit the guns so that's where they went. But I still didn't like the scenario. Four guys could possibly rush Cassidy and take her weapon, and her Spanish wasn't up to keeping track of their conversation if they planned something.

"We'll clear the lighthouse and stick them in there," I said.

Reese checked the door, found it unlocked, and the door swung outward, hinges on the outside. It could be blocked closed. She climbed up the interior quickly, then returned. "One dead guy up top. I tossed his weapon."

It took little convincing to get the four cartel thugs inside, then we blocked the door shut.

Cassidy posted up on the old lighthouse keeper's porch and kept an eye on the door from cover. I still didn't know where Landon was and didn't want her out in the open.

"I told them, anyone comes out, you'll shoot them. If they try it, do it." I said it in Spanish and loud enough that the men inside could hear. Cassidy nodded solemnly.

But when we got around the other side of the lighthouse keeper's place, I signaled Cassidy and had her follow us.

"They won't know you're not still in there for a while. Come on."

"What, you didn't think I'd shoot?"

"Don't worry. There's plenty more shooting to do out here."

Reese and I checked our weapons, then pushed off through the stand of trees to the west. It was only fifty meters till we reached the beach on the opposite side of the island. The only structures were a few thatched-roof gazebos, and a single building with actual walls. It looked like an oversized outhouse, but we had to clear it anyway. I tucked the Colt Python in my waistband and used a two handed grip on my Sig. Reese took point with her M4 while I followed.

We fanned out and cleared the area, but we all came to the same conclusion. He wasn't there.

"Shit. The planes," I said.

We formed up again and started to jog through the brush, around the south end of the compound. We'd almost reached the beach on the other side again.

"Uncle Luke, look out!"

I pivoted as El Halcón stepped out from behind the reliquary chapel and fired three shots. They struck Reese in the chest and leg. I aimed to fire, but he turned, still using Harper as a shield. Her hands were tied behind her and his palm over her mouth. She bit at him and he swore but dragged her back behind the little chapel.

He fired once in my direction before he vanished, but I hit the deck and the shot went high.

Cassidy kept her pistol aimed at the chapel from behind a tree, while I rushed for Reese who was struggling on the ground. I got one arm under her right shoulder and dragged her back a few yards to conceal us behind one of the dormitory buildings.

"Goddamn bastard," Reese muttered as I propped her against the wall. She was wearing her body armor but it hadn't helped with the round that hit her in the hip.

"How bad?" I said.

"Cowardly piece of shit would have been dead quick if he hadn't had a hostage."

"What do you need?"

She pulled a packet of clotting agent from a cargo pocket of her pants and tore it open with her teeth. "I need you to go get that fucker."

El Halcón shouted from beyond the hut. "You and me now, Cabrón. You throw down your guns or the girl dies."

I shouted back. "You won't get out of this if you kill her, Luis. It's over. Your men are all dead. There's no way I let you off this island with the girl." I crept out from behind the dormitory building and worked my way left, farther from Cassidy. If he was going to come out shooting he wouldn't be able to aim two directions at once.

"Guns down now!" he shouted. To my surprise, he sounded frightened. He was a killer, but maybe this was the first time someone had been bold enough to point a gun back. I realized I might be able to intimidate him yet.

"No one else has to die, Luis. Let her go, I swear you walk away from this."

"You never could lie worth a shit," a voice said from behind me. I turned to find Landon ten meters to my left, and he was aiming a gun at my head.

"KNEW I should have found you first," I muttered.

"You've got yourself into what they call an untenable situation," Landon said.

I lowered my weapon a degree and swore.

"I have to give it to you. You almost turned the tables today. What do you think Dad would say if he was here right now?" Landon asked. "Think he'd be proud of what you've managed?"

"I hope not. That would mean I was getting to be too much like you."

"Guess you always did take more after Mom," Landon said. "Hellbent for a tragic ending."

"You want to see tragic, check a mirror sometime."

El Halcón stepped back into view from behind the little chapel and some of the color had come back to his face. He still hadn't let go of Harper though.

"Just shoot that fool already."

Landon ignored him.

Cassidy still had cover behind the tree, but the scenario was shit. She wasn't going to be able to shoot it out with Landon from there and certainly not with both of them. And if I turned around to aim at Landon, either one of them could shoot me.

"You going to do it or what?" El Halcón pressed. And despite the heightened tension of the situation, I had to admit I was curious myself. I let my gun hand fall to my side and turned around to face Landon.

My brother stared at me along the length of his gun barrel. "What do you think of the plane?"

"Engines sounded good. Paint looks like shit."

"A work in progress. Got it out of that damned jungle though."

"You go through all this effort just to make Dad happy?"

"Is that all you ever think of me, little brother?"

"Well, here you are, a drug smuggler, about to let your family die for the sake of profit. Sounds a lot like Dad to me."

Landon's finger twitched on the trigger, but he didn't pull.

"*Tropic Angel* was never his. Not really. It was Mom's."

"Naming it after her didn't make him a less shitty husband."

"Nah. That's true. But she loved it. You were probably too young to remember. She lit up when she was around that old plane. Said it felt like freedom. It was like a symbol. Something she always dreamed about. One of my last good memories of her was standing on the shore of the lake with that plane. She asked me to take her picture with it."

I recalled the photo I'd found in Earl's barn. It had been Landon that gave her that smile.

"Well. I'm glad you had that rosy memory. Doing all this in her honor then? You figure she liked the plane enough to want us pointing guns at each other over it?"

Landon's brow furrowed.

El Halcón removed his gun barrel from Harper's head and aimed it at me. "You going to end this cabrón or what? You can't do it, I'll kill his ass myself."

Harper mumbled something inaudible into his hand.

"We still need him, Luis," Landon said with one hand raised and a new authority in his voice. "More now than before."

"I told you to stop calling me that. Maybe I should shoot you both, huh?" El Halcón's aim pivoted toward Landon.

"I caught some chatter on the radio," Landon countered, meeting his eye. "A local fishing charter saw the explosion and called it in. The authorities are already on their way. We've got two planes to get out of here, and last I checked, you still don't know how to fly. Pablo is dead. We're the only two pilots left. Me and him. You do the math."

I shared a glance with Landon then, and caught the subtle wink he threw me.

Cassidy opened her mouth to say something, but I cut her off with a raised finger. Harper was watching too, she mumbled something else, still muffled by El Halcon's palm, but she looked indignant.

Landon had all the advantages here, but the fact that I was still alive spoke volumes. If he was going to shoot me, he'd have done it already. So what was he up to?

El Halcón wavered.

I dropped my guns in the sand and put my hands up. "Come on out, Cass."

"But—"

"Do you trust me?"

"No! And I trust him even less." She directed the second comment toward Landon. But she slowly lowered her weapon and came out anyway.

El Halcón's expression morphed into a leering grin as Cassidy emerged from behind the tree. Even covered in dirt and sand she still looked better than many women could manage all day.

"Landon still needs a pilot to fly one of these birds. I've got to do it."

She nearly rolled her eyes. Even here on a nearly deserted island we'd found a dude incapable of fathoming women could fly, but El Halcón's oblivious misogyny was keeping me alive right now, so she tossed her gun to the ground.

"And your woman can keep me company until you finish the job," El Halcón said.

Landon and Cassidy were in a staring contest. I knew that look. Cassidy the mind reader. Finally she drew a conclusion. "Fine, let's go then." Her voice was even, but in a tone I recognized as dangerous.

We walked.

My brother and El Halcón kept to the rear with Harper. Cassidy and I were forced to walk up front together.

"Tell me you have a plan," she whispered.

"Taking it moment by moment actually, but maybe we'll get lucky."

"That's not inspiring a lot of confidence."

Crossing the sand we reached *Tropic Angel* first. The plane was angled up the beach, the big engines looming overhead. The tide had risen and now lapped at the bottom of the hull.

The path toward the dock passed under the left wing. Instinctively, I stayed out of the arc of the propeller even though the engine wasn't running. The plane would need to be pushed away from the beach before starting though. The rear hatch was already open and the bags of cash must have been stashed inside. They were no longer in sight on the dock. That explained what Landon had been up to while Cassidy and I were battling cartel guys.

The wreck of the 206 had finally stopped smoldering, but it was a sad sight, missing its wings and listing hard to one side.

Landon pointed to the Grand Caravan still parked at the other side of the dock. "That'll be your ride, Bogey. Cassidy, you'll ride with me in the Mallard. He guided her under the big plane's wing and to the back of the empennage. He then offered her his hand to help her up the Mallard's ladder.

He was getting her out of the way at least.

El Halcón and Harper weren't far from the left engine nacelle. He had followed my path, keeping an eye on me.

Cassidy reached the top of the Mallard's ladder.

"Better sit up front, Cass. You know how you get airsick sometimes in the back," I said.

"No she doesn't," Harper objected. El Halcón's grip on her jaw had slacked and she'd pulled away slightly. He yanked her to him again.

"Hold that thought, Harp," I said. She still looked mad but she clammed up.

Didn't blame her. I was furious too. Days of tension and anger had piled up to the point I was ready to explode. The gunfight had only amplified the feeling. I wasn't denying it anymore.

Cassidy noticed where El Halcón was standing and met my eye, then entered *Tropic Angel*. A moment later I saw her slide into the pilot seat in the flight deck.

If El Halcón noticed, he didn't say anything. He was focused on me.

"How does it feel to lose, Jardínero?" His ego had clearly recovered from the way things had gone so far. And even his arm had stopped bleeding. Apparently his confidence was back to its high water mark too. "You don't get that shipment back to Florida for us quick enough, I'm going to send you little bits of these chicas one piece at a time."

I ventured a look at the Grand Caravan. It would be hauling enough cocaine to put me away for a lifetime if I got caught. But that was only if I survived a worse fate at the hand of Los Tigres.

That's why ending this now was a better idea.

I took a step toward El Halcón, and he tensed and backed away, toward the Mallard.

But I addressed Harper.

"Harp, I've got some good news for you. Your dad's okay."

She wriggled her face free of El Halcón's grip again. "He is?"

"Yeah. His plane and everything. He'll be back to giving you those flying lessons as soon as you get home. Maybe we even give you a ride in a cool bird like this one sometime." I gestured to the Mallard and Harper glanced behind her. Cassidy was watching from the controls and Harper spotted her.

"Little girl ain't going nowhere," El Halcón said. "And I have my doubts you going to see her again."

I took another step toward them and El Halcón backed up again. He was nearly pushed up against the engine nacelle now. He was glaring at me but I focused on Harper instead. I looked her right in the eyes. "This Mallard used to be my mom's plane when I was little. You know the coolest thing about it?"

She shook her head.

"It's the *clear* props."

It took a moment for it to register, but then her eyes widened and she dropped like a rock, ducking so fast El Halcón lost his grip.

Cassidy engaged the starter the same moment and the heavy prop swung around and caught El Halcón in the back. He was knocked forward, tripped, and went to his hands and knees in the sand.

Cassidy hadn't risked using the fuel pump, so the engine hadn't actually started, but it coughed once and puffed out a smoke cloud from the exhaust before going still again.

I was on El Halcón fast. He looked up, eyes wide, and tried to raise his gun, but I punched him hard, connecting with his temple. He went face first into the sand and my momentum carried me into him.

But he still had plenty of fight left. He came up with his shoulder, slamming into me, and we staggered backward, falling into the water together, him partially on top of me.

I gripped the wrist of his gun hand as we went under, ripping at it with my other hand.

It cost me a blow to the face, but he lost his grip on the pistol and it tumbled away in the shallow water. He stretched for it as it fell, but I got my arms around his waist and rolled, carrying us deeper into the surf.

It was only four or five feet deep here, but plenty enough to drown in. We were both under, me now at a disadvantage as I'd pulled El Halcón over me and he was closer to the surface. But every time he tried to plant a foot and get air, I swept his legs from under him with mine and weighed him down, pulling us farther from shore. The underwater wrestling match threatened to drown us both.

If that's what it took, I was game.

But I hadn't counted on the knife. Looked like a switchblade in the single second it took him to pull it from a back pocket. He stuck me in the side before I could get my hands on his wrist.

I writhed in pain but caught his wrist as he pulled the knife loose and plunged it toward me again. The tip of the knife hovered inches from my heart this time.

While El Halcón struggled to impale me again, I scissored his waist with my legs and squeezed.

Bubbles erupted from his open mouth as he shouted in rage under the water.

We sank to the sand, blood tainting the blue around us, still fighting for control of the knife.

Anger distorted his features, but then his expression grew desperate. He was fighting for his life. But that was it.

I had more on the line.

I twisted his wrist and the knife fell from his hand. El Halcón pried at my legs, flailed at my grip on his waist, and dug his nails into my arm. He punched and elbowed my thighs, clawed at my eyes, but I took it, and the blows grew weaker.

I held on. Using less oxygen, just absorbing the hits and letting my weight do the work.

A good pilot keeps his shit together.

More blood drifted from the wound in my side, staining the water crimson, but I didn't let go.

Finally El Halcón's body went limp. A last eruption of bubbles escaped his mouth as his eyes went wide and still.

It had all taken under a minute, but I stayed down till my lungs were screaming, just to be sure.

Finally, chest on fire, I let go of the gangster's body and surfaced.

Cassidy had rushed out of the Mallard and down the loading ladder. She leaped onto the beach and raced for Harper who picked herself up and stumbled to meet her. They crashed together in an embrace, and if Harper would have been able to squeeze the air out of Cass she might have done so with that hug.

My brother stood watching me as I stumbled ashore. I lost my footing and slipped, but before I went down, his hand caught my arm and steadied me.

I stood and looked him in the eye. Wary.

He still had a gun in his other hand. My blurry vision focused on that. He looked down at it too, seeming to notice the weight of it. The implication. But then he dropped the gun in the surf and put his arms around me.

I was slow to embrace him back, but I finally did. It wasn't lost on me that the last time we'd stood like this near *Tropic Angel* we were the kids in that faded polaroid photo. I'd held onto a lot of resentment since then, but the weight of it couldn't stop us from being family. I guess some things never change.

FORTY

DEPARTURE

IT REALLY WASN'T a bad looking beach, if you didn't count the plane debris, the several dead bodies, and the blood I was now dripping into the sand.

Harper released her grip on Cassidy long enough to come wrap her arms around me too. She noticed I was bleeding.

"Are you dying?

"Not today, kiddo."

The wound in my side hadn't penetrated deep. It stung like hell in the salt, and would definitely need stitches or staples, but as far as I could tell, it wasn't going to kill me. My luck had held. I kept pressure on the wound with one hand. "Let's go check on Reese."

Cassidy and Harper walked with me as we made our way back up the beach toward the dormitories. Reese called to us from the wall of the little chapel as we approached. She'd evidently crawled there. "You need me to shoot that dumb brother of yours?"

"Maybe later." I eyed her newly bandaged hip. "You think you can stand?"

She put a hand up and I grasped her wrist, hoisting her to her good leg. She winced but made it look cool.

"By the way. I'll take that raise in my next paycheck."

I laughed. "You've set a high bar for the next employee evaluations."

Cassidy picked up the M4 for Reese and we moved back toward the beach.

Landon met us partway.

"It would be nice to have a longer reunion, Bogey, but I wasn't lying about that radio chatter. Those DEA boats won't take long getting out here. We've gotta fly."

I took a look at the end of the dock and the ruin of my slowly sinking 206. "My ride is missing a few key pieces."

He held out a small keychain with a red "Remove Before Flight" float on it. Looked like a cabin door key.

"The Caravan?"

"No, brother. I want you to take *Tropic Angel*. It's time for her to go home."

I accepted the key. "You aren't coming with us."

"Well, there's forty million in coke in that Caravan. The feds get it, La Reina Tigre comes for all of our heads. If I deliver it, maybe she won't."

"We left a lot of her men dead on this beach either way."

"She's not going to love you for that. But she might actually respect you a bit more. There's worse bargaining situations."

"Your knowledge of drug lords thus far has not been my favorite part of our relationship."

"We're walking different roads, Bogey. Always have. I never was cut out for yours. Though I am starting to see the benefits." He was looking at the women beside me when he said that. Cassidy had her arm around Harper. Reese had one hand on my shoulder, helping her balance.

"Will you run back to Mexico after?" I asked. "Where's this road end?"

"You'll see me around."

"Is that a promise or a threat?" Cassidy asked.

Landon gave her a smile. "Don't expect me to darken your doorstep anytime soon."

"You've got the money?" I asked.

"I put half in the Caravan. Other half is in the Mallard. Hold onto it for me, will you?" Landon asked. "I get this product offloaded, I'll still need a bargaining chip with La Reina Tigre. Helps if it's not all in the same place."

"We don't need targets on our heads. Keep your money."

"I do owe you a plane. Reimburse yourself if you like. The boss isn't hurting for cash. She's after other assets."

"I'm not giving her more planes."

"I know. You're not cut out for this any more than I am for your life. But don't worry about it. I'll find her what she needs someplace else."

"Business as usual."

"Always costs something. Got *her* back though, didn't I?" His eyes lingered on *Tropic Angel*. "Keep her safe for me. Maybe get her some fresh paint while you're at it." He backed away toward the dock. In the distance I caught the sound of boat motors.

We both looked to the southern horizon. Our time was up.

Pushing the Mallard off the beach was the hardest bit, but once it was floating, we pulled it around to the dock to load up. Cassidy found the M20 where Reese had left it and we gathered what other evidence we could of our visit onto the plane as the police boats neared.

I cut the 206 loose and it slowly drifted away from the dock as it continued to sink. It could join the other wrecks claimed by Scorpion Reef.

Landon fired up the Grand Caravan and taxied away from the dock with a wave.

Climbing aboard *Tropic Angel* was a plunge into my memory. The smell of the seats, the feel of my fingers on the overhead throttles. But it was no time for nostalgia. We got the starboard engine started, then pushed off and Harper closed the boarding hatch before strapping in across from Reese in one of only two remaining passenger seats.

The approaching police boats sent up a signal flare and we were hailed via a bullhorn, but I had both engines running now and was plowing through light waves in the opposite direction. The boats chased us, but where we were going, they couldn't follow. As we gained speed, I eased back on the yoke and *Tropic Angel* lifted clear of the water, the vibration of the big engines making my fingertips quiver. We stayed low over the water to pick up airspeed, then climbed, up and around. Isla Pérez and the beauty of the coral reef below passed aft out the starboard windows.

Cassidy looked over at me from the copilot seat and smiled. The first real smile I'd seen on her in a while. And I'd missed seeing it.

Northeast.

We flew in shifts. Cass had the controls while I checked on Reese's bullet wound. Reese taped my cut up with butterfly bandages and some super glue we found in the plane's first aid kit.

Even Harper had a chance in the copilot seat so Cass could get some well-deserved rest in the back. Cassidy had slept the least in the last thirty-six hours, and despite insisting she wouldn't be able to rest, was passed out in minutes.

It was dark well before we reached the coast of Florida, but nighttime traffic still flew. I approached with lights out and transponder off till I reached the shoreline, then flipped the lights and transponder on and entered the traffic pattern at Everglades City. I flew two circuits before heading north, repeating the process at several other small airports, squawking a VFR transponder code and blending in among other innocent radar traffic. The ID on the transponder Landon had installed likely didn't match the plane, but I was surprised he'd even bothered to put one in. Eventually, I made my way to Lake Okeechobee and landed on the broad expanse of fresh water.

If we'd aroused the suspicions of the DEA or air traffic control, they'd be looking at airports first and unlikely to find us out here.

I dropped an anchor out the front nose hatch and Harper and I climbed onto the wings to stretch our legs and look at stars overhead.

We talked about her dad and how he'd flown to Cancún as part of the plan to save her. I left out the parts of the story that implicated her parents in a theft. That was their job to explain it to her. But I had a feeling she already grasped the general situation.

"You think my parents will be okay?" she asked. "They've really screwed each other up."

"Hard to say what's going to happen. I know they were terrified of losing you. But sometimes a little trouble makes a family more resilient. Could be that your parents have found more to fight for in their marriage than they realized. Who knows, you all might come out of this stronger."

"All of us?" she said, reaching out and tugging on the friendship bracelet I still wore.

I put an arm around her shoulder and squeezed. "Especially the godparents."

A little while after Harper got tired and went back in,

Cassidy found me. She climbed out the nose hatch and I helped her up to the top of the plane. We didn't talk much, but I pointed out the constellations I knew and told her a couple of the old stories my mother had made up about them.

I wondered aloud what she would have thought about her favorite plane finally coming back to these waters.

"I think she'd like you being here thinking about her most of all," Cassidy said. "I do regret that I never got a chance to meet her. Sounds like the kind of woman I would have liked."

"She would have liked you too. She loved meeting other women who flew. She said women belonged in the heavens because they were natural-born angels."

"I might have more work to do on that front," Cassidy said.

"You're doing pretty well in my opinion."

She stroked the aluminum wing beneath her. "Maybe you and I could be a restoration project too." Her hand found mine and our eyes met. Then she leaned over and kissed me.

I kissed her back.

We laid on top of that wing staring at stars together for another hour, till I finally started drifting off.

We all managed a couple hours of sleep on the floor of the Mallard before waking to the pre-dawn light. I fired up the old engines and we took off before the sun was up. We flew direct to Albert Whitted, staying under Tampa's airspace, skimming the bay and landing on runway 25 before the control tower at Whitted officially opened at seven.

Just like the plane, we were tired and thirsty and beat up. But we were finally home.

FORTY-ONE

TRUE MAGNUM

A COUPLE DAYS LATER, Detective Blake Rivers sat in the office chair across the desk from mine and studied the Post-it note I'd handed to her. It listed a name and phone number.

"You're referring me to this woman?"

"It won't be Marie specifically, but her firm in general. The Carters became clients of theirs recently, and they advised everyone in the family to use their services whenever the need arose."

"Recently, as in whenever it was you got back from wherever it was you disappeared to after I told you not to go anywhere?"

I shrugged. I'd gotten good at shrugging lately.

I'd shrugged at questions like: Why are you moving so stiffly? Where is your Cessna 206? Why is there a Grumman Mallard in your hangar? Actually, that one I'd blamed on an imaginary customer. Just in for some repairs. Needed a new transponder for sure. Probably some paint work and a new registration number.

I'd shrugged at a few questions about the Carters too. Did I really believe the story Chris had told about being in Cancún the whole time he was missing? Just faking a disappearance to make

Ava miss him. What had Ava really been up to with Johnny Garbanza? I shrugged off questions about why Reese was on a surprise paid staycation this week too. My shoulders were getting a workout.

Chris and Ava would possibly face jail time or fines for the misdemeanor of filing a false police report, but they hadn't actually submitted an insurance claim, so they'd likely dodge the fraud charges.

Detective Rivers hadn't given any indication that the police were aware of the five million in cash that went missing from Johnny's place so I hadn't needed to shrug about that, or the fact that half of it was currently stashed on the roof of my office in a duffel bag roughly eight feet over her head. I hadn't been dumb enough to spend any of it. I'd likely stick it in a dusty barn in Central Florida for a while, till I found a more permanent solution to my issues with La Reina Tigre. It wasn't money I wanted any association with, and the faster it was out of my life, the better.

I *had* turned all the pistols registered in my name over to Detective Rivers. Her forensics department had confirmed that the bullet that killed Johnny Garbanza wasn't from any of my guns. They found plenty of salt water residue though.

Detective Rivers kept her sharp eyes on me while she spoke. "Camera footage retrieved from Mr. Garbanza's house has shown that the men you described did reenter his home around the time of his death. One of the men was identified as a Mexican national named Luis 'El Halcón' Carrasquillo. He's got quite the rap sheet, including running an illegal dogfighting ring in Tampa. If you encounter him again, we'd really like to know about it."

"I'd be surprised to see him again. You'll be my first call if I do."

Detective Rivers was no dummy. She knew I had more information than I was letting on, but Chris Carter was back, evidently not murdered, and she had other actual homicide cases to worry about. She petted Murphy on her way out and his tail wagged. He liked her. I did too when I thought about it, but I was fine if she wanted us to not visit each other professionally anymore.

We'd have to see.

After work, Murphy and I drove to Reese's place in the Wrangler. It was hot and the humidity felt like a wet blanket, but riding around St. Pete never failed to put me in a good mood, no matter the weather. I'd lost my lucky shades on Scorpion Reef, but I found a new pair of aviators in the liquor store when I stopped for supplies. I wore those as I drove the rest of the way, and they gave the city a golden glow.

I'd brought along a gift bag stuffed with tissue paper and set it on Reese's kitchen counter with the liquor store purchases after I walked in. Reese was on the couch.

"What's the latest from the doctors?" I asked while I rummaged around her liquor cabinet for a mixing cup.

"They're finally done poking at me. Still debating if I'll need surgery. For now it's all physical therapy."

"Any long-term damage?" I found a couple of cocktail glasses and filled them with ice.

"I'm probably out of the running as a future ballet dancer. But I'll manage." She pushed herself off the couch and stretched before limping over to join me in the kitchen.

"Hope you are in the market for a margarita, because that's what I brought."

"You have my interest."

I finished shaking the ingredients up and poured one for Reese first.

She eased herself onto a stool. "What's the latest with the Carter clan?"

"Ava and Chris are selling their place. Moving back to Boston with her parents for a bit till they get back on their feet financially." I slid her the drink. "They don't seem to be headed for prison yet, but they're bankrupt."

"Getting away with it?"

"Not everyone who deserves a comeuppance always gets what they deserve. But luck like that doesn't last."

"Sucks they have to relocate. Harper seemed amped to get in more flying with you."

"We'll get her back down here eventually. Cass has a few airline passes to burn. There's a couple of new bracelets in that bag from Harper by the way. You're officially in her friends club."

"That's sweet of her."

She sipped her margarita and gave me a thumbs up. "What's with you and Cassidy now?"

"To be determined. She's headed back to Boston for a bit too, to help out. I think Harper could use the stability. But who knows. We decided to buy Dale out of his share of Archangel. Cass will be the only other owner in the owners meetings from now on."

"You were up on the roof of that plane together for a while. Don't think I didn't notice."

"A woman's heart is a wild and mysterious place. Should I discover any of its secrets, you'll be the first to hear about it."

She scoffed, then yanked the tissue paper from the gift bag before pulling out the blue baseball cap.

"Detroit Tigers?" But then she smiled. "Because of Tom Selleck."

"That action you pulled off on Scorpion Reef was some true Magnum shit. Figured you earned the hat to prove it."

She inspected the hat appreciatively, then paused when she saw the snap back. "Adjustable?"

"Well, just in case there's further debate."

She laughed, then put the cap on backwards. "What other

trouble do you think we'll possibly get into that could ever top this one?"

I grinned. "I don't know. But I'm kinda looking forward to finding out."

———

Thanks for reading and enjoying this adventure! Ready for more? Be sure to check out the bonus epilogue, bonus beach scene chapter and get on the list to be notified of the next release in this series.

Get book 2.
TROPIC DESCENT
https://mybook.to/Archangel-Aviation

You can read the bonus epilogue, bonus beach chapter, and another deleted scene in the bonus content here:

https://BookHip.com/TZTFAKW

If you enjoyed this book, **please leave it a review**! You can also follow Nate Van Coops on Amazon or Goodreads to be notified of future books.

ACKNOWLEDGMENTS

This book was a lot of fun to write and I hope you enjoyed the read!

Having been in aviation for over twenty years and writing for more than a decade, it probably should have occurred to me to write an aviation thriller before now, but I'm happy to bring all that combined experience to this series and deliver the best book I know how to produce.

No book happens in a vacuum. I'm eternally indebted to my fellow writers, Alan Lee, T. Ellery Hodges, Lucy Score, Bella Michaels, Boo Walker, and James Blatch for their advice around the virtual water cooler that kept me motivated and encouraged.

I'm grateful to have had my parents, Marilyn and Kevin Bourdeau, who believed in my dreams enough to put me in an airplane at fifteen, and for hiding in that barn to take pictures on the day of my first solo.

Thanks for sending me to flight school against daunting odds, and being a source of constant encouragement even when I decided to become a mechanic too, and was at the time, "not very mechanical."

Mom, you've read everything I've written more times than I have and it fills my heart so full that I'm always excited to write the next one for you.

I'm blessed to have accumulated some amazing readers over the years and a select group have become The Type Pros, who test fly everything I write and clean it up for public consumption.

You all make me look good, and I love having you on my team. Specific thanks to Mark Hale, Maarja Kruusmets, Judy Eiler, Eric Lizotte, Ken Robbins, Felicia Rodriguez, Claire Manger, Ginelle Blanch, Sarah Van Coops-Bush, and Bethany Cousins.

Most of this book was written sitting in the seat I often occupy in the Driftwood Kava and Roastery, whose staff have been infinitely patient with the amount of hours I take up table space. Thanks to Julian, Cassidy, Jeff and all the other staff for keeping me highly caffeinated. My heart beats faster for you.

My final thanks always goes to my family, my children Piper and Morgan whose hugs and smiles make my life, and my beautiful wife Stephanie for always being more on top of things, more conventionally employed, and more socially charming than I can ever hope to be. I married way out of my league when I snagged you, and I hope you never realize it.

ABOUT THE AUTHOR

NATE VAN COOPS is a commercial pilot, mechanic, and certified flight instructor in St. Petersburg Florida. His addictions to tacos and pickle ball wage a war for supremacy daily. When not writing, or flying at his favorite airport, you'll find him e-biking around St. Pete with his wife and kids. He also writes science fiction books under the name Nathan Van Coops. Learn more at nathanvancoops.com.

To say hello, or to inquire about the availability of film or television rights, send email to: nathan@nathanvancoops.com

Made in United States
North Haven, CT
18 October 2024

59115408R00157